"Did you do it, Carly? Did you help take the money?" Dan pressed.

"No," Carly replied. She sat with her hands in her lap, looking at him stonily.

It was all he could do to hang tough. "Why did you leave with Tony?"

"We were going on a weekend cruise in Mazatlán."

"But you ended up on Isla Linda. Apparently that cruise wasn't what it seemed."

"A lot of things weren't as they seemed—including Tony. I'm a slow learner, you see. It's taken me some time to realize that men can't be trusted."

Women, either, Dan wanted to shout, catching himself just in time.

"Why did you run from me, then?"

Carly shrugged. "For one thing, I thought my stepfather might have sent you to keep me here so he could get my trust fund."

"And for another?"

"For another, I th
window, even thou
glass reflected the s
Dan watched Carly'
I was in love with yo

Dear Reader,

Whether it's a vacation fling in some far-off land, or falling for the guy next door, there's something irresistible about summer romance. This month, we have an irresistible lineup for you, ranging from sunny to sizzling.

We continue our FABULOUS FATHERS series with *Accidental Dad* by Anne Peters. Gerald Marsden is not interested in being tied down! But once he finds himself the temporary father of a lonely boy, *and* the temporary husband of his lovely landlady, Gerald wonders if he might not actually enjoy a permanent role as "family man."

Marie Ferrarella, one of your favorite authors, brings us a heroine who's determined to settle down—but not with a man who's always rushing off to another archaeological site! However, when Max's latest find shows up *In Her Own Backyard,* Rikki makes some delightful discoveries of her own....

The popular Phyllis Halldorson returns to Silhouette Romance for a special story about reunited lovers who must learn to trust again, in *More Than You Know.* Kasey Michaels brings her bright and humorous style to a story of love at long distance in the enchanting *Marriage in a Suitcase.*

Rounding out July are two stories that simmer with passion and deception—*The Man Behind the Magic* by Kristina Logan and *Almost Innocent* by Kate Bradley.

In the months to come, look for more titles by your favorite authors—including Diana Palmer, Elizabeth August, Suzanne Carey, Carla Cassidy and many, many more!

Happy reading!

Anne Canadeo
Senior Editor

ALMOST INNOCENT

Kate Bradley

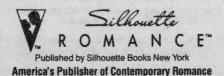

Silhouette
ROMANCE™
Published by Silhouette Books New York
America's Publisher of Contemporary Romance

SILHOUETTE BOOKS
300 East 42nd St., New York, N.Y. 10017

ALMOST INNOCENT

Copyright © 1993 by Kathleen Bryant

All rights reserved. Except for use in any review, the reproduction or utilization of this work in whole or in part in any form by any electronic, mechanical or other means, now known or hereafter invented, including xerography, photocopying and recording, or in any information storage or retrieval system, is forbidden without the permission of the publisher, Silhouette Books, 300 E. 42nd St., New York, N.Y. 10017

ISBN: 0-373-08951-1

First Silhouette Books printing July 1993

All the characters in this book have no existence outside the imagination of the author and have no relation whatsoever to anyone bearing the same name or names. They are not even distantly inspired by any individual known or unknown to the author, and all incidents are pure invention.

®: Trademark used under license and registered in the United States Patent and Trademark Office and in other countries.

Printed in the U.S.A.

KATE BRADLEY

is wild about baseball, the blues, Bette Davis movies and—of course—books. Born in Minnesota, she is currently thawing out in the Arizona desert.

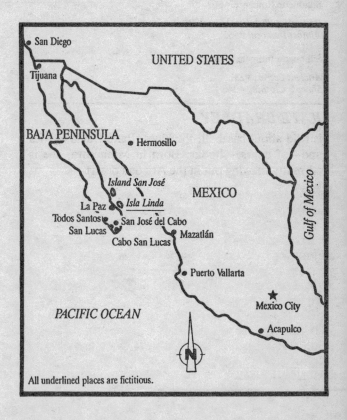

All underlined places are fictitious.

Prologue

For an entire weekend she slept and tried to forget. Sounds drifted in and out of her dreams—the hushed giggles and melodious Spanish of the maids in the hallway, the raspy brush of palm leaves in the ocean breeze, the low, rhythmic murmur of the ocean. Carly Dawson slept through it all, waking only briefly to use the small bathroom that adjoined her room, then to shuffle back to the bed that promised oblivion.

But the oblivion didn't last. When she awoke late Monday morning, she was still Carly Dawson, twenty-three years old, of Phoenix, Arizona. Only she wasn't in Arizona any more. She was a world away on Isla Linda, a small island off Baja California.

And she was alone.

Unable to hide from the truth any longer, Carly sat up and rubbed her swollen eyelids, wondering if she would ever learn to see through a man's lies. Gullibility seemed to be a family trait, passed along like a defective gene from her mother, Claire Cheswick-Dawson, whose film career had

ranked a distant second to her career of trusting the wrong
men.

As a pang of hunger forced her further into the reality of
her surroundings, Carly tried to remember the last time
she'd interrupted her bout of self-indulgent moping to eat.
The congealed remnants of a room-service meal sat on a tray
by the door. She wrinkled her nose in distaste and got out of
bed, reaching for the suitcase she'd never bothered to un-
pack.

She shoved aside the bright sundresses and brief swim-
suits until she found a pair of navy slacks and a matching
blouse. She donned them mechanically, noting her hollow
cheeks and dull blue eyes in the mirror above the ornately
carved chest of drawers. Only her shoulder-length hair
seemed alive, its auburn highlights undimmed by her ill
spirits. She ran a comb through it halfheartedly and went
downstairs in search of something to eat.

The Paloma Rosa was the only hotel on tiny Isla Linda,
Tony had told her as they arrived from the mainland three
days ago. It was, he'd promised, a romantic hideaway of
Colonial charm and seaside luxury.

Carly hesitated in the doorway of the hotel's balcony café.
Tall palms and deep pink bougainvillea framed a postcard-
perfect view of the Sea of Cortez, the band of water that
separated the Baja Peninsula from the Mexican mainland.
The beauty was lost on her.

"Ah, *señorita . . .* "

A stocky, middle-aged man bustled over to her, speaking
in rumbling Spanish. She didn't understand a word, but the
concern in his brown eyes was evident. He was the owner,
who had checked them into the hotel late Friday night and
witnessed her objections on learning that Tony had reserved only one room. And now he obviously knew that
Tony had deserted her.

Uncomfortable that this stranger had seen how gullible and stupid she was, Carly reminded him coolly, "I don't speak Spanish."

"That's all right, *señorita*. My English is very good." He beamed at her reassuringly. "Come this way, please. You will sit by the view. A little sunshine would be good, *sí?*"

His kindness was almost more than she could bear. She followed him to the linen-covered table and sat down. He put a menu in her hands, and she stared at it helplessly. Even if she could read Spanish, she wasn't ready to make even the smallest of decisions.

"May I?" He took the menu from her. "I will bring you something special," he said. He gestured toward a pretty young woman wearing a dove gray waitress uniform. "This is Aña," he introduced. "She will help you now. My name is Paolo."

Carly thanked him and smiled politely as the waitress filled her glass with orange juice.

"*Jugo de naranja,*" Aña said helpfully.

Carly repeated the phrase and smiled politely, although she would have rather been alone. Aña seemed to understand this, for she came and went quietly from then on, bringing a small pot of coffee and cream, a basket of fresh sweet rolls, a plate of fruit, and a folded-up American newspaper, before leaving Carly to her self-reproach.

Carly had met Tony Williamson six months ago, when he had started at Security National as an investment banker. She'd just been awarded her own list of clients the week before, and Tony's willingness to share his knowledge and experience had won her gratitude. Remembering how she had looked up to him, she smiled bitterly.

Tony had teased her about her overwhelming desire to succeed. It was common knowledge that Carly's late mother had been a famous actress and that her stepfather, Robert Daimler, was one of the largest land developers in Maricopa County. But Carly wanted nothing from her stepfather, and she longed for the day sixteen months from now when she would turn twenty-five and gain full control of the trust fund left to her by her mother, now controlled by Robert Daimler.

Which had made things that much easier for Tony....

Seven years her senior, Tony had gone from being a mentor to a colleague, and then to something more. They'd worked together on a number of accounts, and when he'd asked her to go away with him for a three-day weekend in Mazatlán, Mexico, Carly had considered it an opportunity for them to get to know each other better outside of the office, where they had to be discreet.

The trip to Mexico had been magical. They'd slipped out of the office early Friday afternoon, giggling like conspirators, driving in Tony's elegant BMW to the airport. When they'd taken another flight from Mazatlán to La Paz, Carly hadn't questioned the sudden change in plans. As they drove up the Baja California coastline, Tony told her about the paradise that awaited them on Isla Linda.

He hadn't told Carly that he'd planned on sharing her room.

That had been the first shock. Although she'd believed she was falling in love with him, she hardly knew him. She hadn't even told him about her past, the reason that she seemed "older than her years," as Tony had commented on more than one occasion. *Another mistake, another male.* And because of that mistake, she had to wait until she turned twenty-five to gain control of her trust fund. Her past had made her cautious, and she wasn't about to throw caution to the wind to share a bed with Tony.

She'd explained with deep embarrassment that perhaps she might change her mind by the end of the weekend, once they got to know each other a little better. Tony had been angry at her excuse. With the nervous desk clerk looking on, he'd called Carly an ugly name, and started shouting so loudly that the clerk had summoned the hotel's owner.

Paolo had discreetly intervened, telling Tony that another, adjoining room was available due to a late cancellation, and that he was able to offer it at a discount. Tony had taken both rooms, ungraciously. As they'd walked down the hallway behind Paolo, he'd kept a tight grip above Carly's elbow.

She rubbed the area, remembering. Paolo had left them, and Tony had continued his taunts. It was then that she discovered the worst. Tony was married. He had laughed at her naïveté, and she'd begged him to take her home. *Too late,* he'd told her. They would leave in the morning. But when she woke up Saturday morning, the room next to hers was empty. Tony had gone, and she spent the rest of the weekend wallowing in self-recrimination and shame.

Poor little rich girl. How many times had she been taunted with that phrase? Her mother's money had drawn every fortune hunter like a magnet, and Carly's childhood was filled with a string of "daddies." Robert Daimler was the last, and the *worst.* At sixteen, Carly had rebelled by looking for trouble and finding it with a bunch of tough kids led by an eighteen-year-old named Scott. Desperate to fit in and prove that she was like them, not a rich princess with everything, she'd let Scott and his cohorts lead her into one mess after another. Finally, a concerned teacher had suggested that Claire Cheswick-Dawson send her daughter away to a disciplinary academy.

Carly had worked hard to show that the trouble she'd gotten into with Scott and his cohorts as a teenager was behind her. She'd graduated from the academy and gone on to college, but her mother had died from an aneurysm before Carly could prove herself.

Of course, Robert had undermined Carly's efforts at every turn, using the friction between them to create her mother's doubts. Because of his machinations, the breach between mother and daughter had never completely healed.

And now, Carly realized, she'd made another mistake. When would she learn that, like her mother, she couldn't trust her judgment when it came to men? She swallowed and closed her eyes, fighting back frustrated tears. Slowly, she became aware of the sea breeze that lifted her hair and brushed over her bare arms, the scent of the pineapple Aña had brought, the sound of children laughing on the beach. She opened her eyes again, knowing she couldn't hide out here any longer.

She had to return to Phoenix and face the knowing looks of her fellow employees, the "I told you so" from her step-father. For once, Robert Daimler was right. He'd warned Carly that Tony was trouble, and she hadn't listened. Facing Robert would be hard, harder even than facing the people at the bank.

She hadn't lived in the house on Camelback Mountain since her mother's death three years ago, but Robert Daimler had done what he could to make her life miserable. This time, she refused to ask him for help, even though she had little cash with her. She was sure she could use her credit card for the hotel bill, and get an advance to pay for a ferry to the mainland. She'd call her friend Jill, a law student at Arizona State University, and ask her to meet her on the coast and drive her back to Phoenix. Maybe Robert wouldn't even find out what had happened, she thought hopefully.

Her hopes died when she picked up the folded newspaper and stared at the headline: Embezzlement! Partners in Crime Steal Millions and Head for the Border.

Her heart pounding, she read how a Phoenix investment banker had laundered millions of dollars, manipulated accounts and, with the help of a co-worker, escaped to Mexico with two million in negotiable bonds. She recognized Tony's name.

And hers.

A half-dozen images flashed through her mind, things that had seemed innocent or insignificant at the time: Tony's sly hint to the receptionist that he and Carly were going away together, the phone call he'd taken at Carly's desk and his hurried request to use her workstation moments before they left, the haste to get to the airport, the last-minute decision to come to Isla Linda instead of staying in Mazatlán.

Now it all made sense. With his assurance and skill, Tony had pulled the wool over everyone's eyes. He'd obviously spent the last six months laundering money for others, then topped it off by taking two million for himself. Normally, the discrepancies wouldn't be found until the end-of-month audit, but Tony must have forgotten that the Management Information System department had spent the weekend clearing off the network to create more space.

With a sinking feeling in the pit of her stomach, Carly knew that Tony had used her computer to open a bogus account so that the transaction would be traced back to her password and her user pathway on the network. And she also knew that her troubles were only beginning.

Chapter One

Isla Linda, Mexico. Ten months later.

"Hey, baby, how about it? Wanna come back to the boat with us for some fun and games?"

Carly pretended not to hear the taunt from the table of rowdy young men she was serving. They'd arrived shortly after sunset, and now, three hours and several rounds later, they were loud and drunk. In her months of working in the cantina, situations like this one had been thankfully infrequent. But it was spring break, and now and then restless college students migrated by boat or ferry from Los Cabos or somewhere on the mainland. Finding the tiny island too quiet and tame for their tastes, they would either move on or, as in this case, create their own excitement.

They continued their verbal assault as she picked up empty beer bottles and glasses—dead soldiers, as the rowdy boys termed them—and set them on her serving tray. She carried the loaded tray back to the bar, tuning out their increasingly distasteful remarks. She found it hard to believe that she'd ever been that young. When she was their age, she'd been working so hard trying to regain her mother's faith that she never would have considered acting up the way these boys were. And yet now, older and wiser, she'd somehow managed to land herself in even deeper trouble.

Carly's brief bout of self-pity was chased away by anger as a voice called loudly, "Hey, *chiquita*. Why don't you come back here and make me happy?" A chorus of approving laughter followed the remark.

As she unloaded the tray's contents, the bartender, Luis, asked Carly if she wanted him to take over the table. He lowered his voice as he spoke, although she doubted that the group of obnoxious boys understood Spanish outside of an occasional word, which they badly mispronounced.

"I'll handle it," she assured Luis, striving for confidence. One thing she'd learned was not to count on anyone except herself. Her mother had let her down by marrying Robert and taking his side over hers. Scott and his friends had used her in their exploits against the law. And Tony had tried to frame her. The latest disappointment was her attorney, who had decided two weeks ago to withdraw from her case, destroying months of progress and dashing her hopes to return to the U.S. any time soon.

Stop feeling sorry for yourself, she scolded, trying to concentrate on her demanding customers. Her impatience with them grew. Didn't they know how lucky they were, able to go home whenever they wanted, without having to worry about being arrested and charged with a felony?

She took the beers and drinks back to the table and suffered through several suggestive remarks from two of the rowdiest boys. They spurred each other on, each trying to outdo the other with how far he could push Carly. When the taller one placed his hand on her backside, she decided that she'd had enough. She was tired of Isla Linda, tired of laying low to avoid the authorities. And she was tired of being treated like an object to be pushed around.

She picked up the rum and cola he'd ordered and very deliberately held it above his lap, noting with satisfaction that the baggy cotton shorts he was wearing left his skinny, sunburnt legs bare. For one reckless moment, she didn't care about consequences.

She turned the glass upside down, told him in perfect colloquial Spanish to go screw himself, and then waited for all hell to break loose.

As he watched the events transpiring at the table across the dimly lit, smoke-hazed room, Dan Turner considered himself a lucky man. He'd spent months looking for Tony Williamson and his partner. When he got the tip that Carly Dawson had been hiding out on an island off Baja California as recently as a few weeks ago, he figured it would take him another week at least to track her down.

But here she was in the first place he'd looked. Her dark hair was much shorter than in the old photo he'd been carrying around, her skin tanned and smooth. She could speak Spanish like a native, and she fixed a mean margarita, he acknowledged with an appreciative sip.

But she was obviously not a street brawler.

He put down his glass, stood, and crossed the room with a quickness that belied his indolent demeanor. The lanky kid had Carly by both wrists, and the shorter one was coming around the table to stand behind her. He never made it. Dan grabbed him by the collar with one hand, barely hearing the bottles and glasses crash to the floor as the kid reached out wildly in order to steady himself. Dan used his other hand to grasp Carly's tormenter by the neck, and the lanky kid immediately dropped his hold on her arms.

"I don't think the lady appreciates your attentions," Dan said.

Out of the corner of his eye, he could see the bartender—Luis, he'd heard Carly call him—slipping through a doorway behind the carved wooden bar. Dan figured the man could be going into the back office for a gun, but he suspected that Luis was heading out the back door instead. None of the other patrons had noticed the fleeing bartender. The minute Dan had shoved his chair back, all conversation had ceased and all heads turned to him.

"Yeah, well, we were getting along just fine until you stuck your nose into it," the lanky one said, his voice strangled.

Dan relaxed his hold a bit. The tension in the room was so electric, it rose the hairs on the back of his neck. He sensed that the crowd, locals and fishermen, was on his side. He wasn't worried about losing a fight. He just didn't want it to get that far.

"Didn't look that way to me," Dan said easily. "How about it?"

He turned to Carly Dawson, looking at her directly for the first time since he'd crossed the room. She had the biggest, deepest blue eyes he'd ever seen, and all the air went out of his lungs at the sight. If he didn't know better, he'd swear that Lanky had sucker-punched him in the gut.

After looking at her photograph for the past few weeks, he thought he knew her face as well as his own. But the black-and-white picture hadn't prepared him for her jewel blue eyes or the fiery highlights in her dark hair. It was a good thing the other three boys had judiciously decided to remain in their seats, and that the two he was holding on to hadn't put up much of a struggle. He had a feeling an entire army could have marched through the bar during those moments and he wouldn't have noticed. He realized that she was staring as hard as he was, and he repeated his question.

"How about it? Were these guys bothering you?"

"Yes they were, but I thought I'd managed to put out the fire," she said, her voice low and precise, as though she wasn't used to speaking in English.

"Well, some fires burn hotter than others."

Dan looked down at the puddle of cola and ice melting in front of the kid's feet. As his gaze lifted, he saw that Carly was rubbing her wrists where Lanky had grabbed her. "Are you sure you're okay?" he asked.

"It's nothing," she said. The brightness of her blue eyes belied her words. Dan felt a rush of protectiveness and quickly shoved it aside. Carly Dawson was a hustling little tramp, and he'd better remember it.

Angry at his lapse, he shook both of the culprits he still held in his grasp. "What about it, boys—ready to call it a night?"

The one he held by the collar nodded as the three at the table quietly put down several bills, got up, and left. Dan let him go and concentrated on Lanky. The young man's expression was still defiant as he stared up at Dan.

"Excuse us," Dan said to Carly.

He guided Lanky away from the table, still holding on to the boy's neck. He pretended not to notice the rapt audience that watched his every move as he tapped the university logo on Lanky's T-shirt and said, "Looks like they're teaching you how to be stupid at that college you go to, kid. Think of tonight as a brief lesson in life."

"Oh yeah?"

Dan recognized the nervousness behind the challenging response. He lowered his head to the boy's ear and warned, "You'd better learn to show a little respect, or someday you're gonna end up in a lot more trouble than this." He finished with a few low-voiced threats directly into Lanky's ear. His lecture over, Dan released the boy.

Lanky looked away from Dan's stinging gaze toward Carly, who was busy clearing the mess of glass and spilt liquor on the table and floor.

Dan tensed as Lanky walked toward Carly, ready to grab the kid again and this time give him the walloping he deserved. But Lanky stopped a respectable distance away from her, looking over his shoulder at Dan for a brief moment before he spoke.

"I'm sorry, ma'am," he told Carly before turning and walking out of the bar.

Dan walked over to where Carly was standing, a look of bemusement on her face. "Are you gonna be okay?" he asked her.

"I'm fine," she said. "Thanks," she added, almost awkwardly. Dan realized she was uncomfortable standing there with all eyes on her.

"Here, let me take that for you," he offered, reaching out for the tray covered with broken glass. "Sorry about the mess," he added as she followed him to the bar.

"I have a feeling it would have been much worse if you hadn't intervened," she said. "What did you say to him, anyway?"

"Just a few simple truths," Dan answered as he set the tray on the bar.

"Well, thanks again for your help—" She stopped. "I just realized I don't even know your name."

"Dan Turner," he told her.

"I'm Carly," she said, reaching out to shake his hand. Dan resisted the impulse to hold on any longer than necessary.

"I saw the bartender leave," he told her. "Why don't you close up and let me walk you home?"

"There's no need," she said. "Really, I am fine." She bent down to pick up the last shard of glass, dismissing him.

"They could be waiting outside for you," he told her, unwilling to give up so easily. "I didn't give them the fight they were spoiling for, and they might just be looking for a little more trouble yet tonight."

She sighed. "Look, I appreciate what you did, but I don't even know you. I'd be pretty stupid going home with someone I'd just met even to avoid a bunch of rowdy boys. I might be jumping from the frying pan into the fire," she said.

Dan couldn't argue with her logic. He thought of the reason he'd come to Isla Linda. With grim amusement he acknowledged that Carly Dawson was probably safer with a bunch of boys than she was with him. But he had a job to do, and getting closer to Carly Dawson was part of it.

He was about to try again to convince her, but she left him standing at the bar and began clearing the remaining tables, where a few die-hard customers still lingered. Deprived of what had looked to be a promising rumble, they were reluctant to leave.

"Bar's closed," Carly told them in Spanish. A couple of them grumbled before heading for the exit. Carly held the door open as the last one passed through, then looked pointedly at Dan. "You still here?" she asked.

He wanted to talk to her, to get this mission of his over with, but one look at her determined expression told him it would be useless to argue.

"Just leaving," he said affably as he stepped out the door. It shut firmly behind him, leaving him standing alone in the small gravel parking lot bordered by a palm grove on one side and the entrance to the marina on the other. He scanned the area, searching the shadows for any sign of the college boys. He saw no cars, but he spotted the tiny glow of a cigarette near a palm tree.

He walked toward the grove of palms, and the unseen observer broke into a run. Dan quickly caught up and grabbed at the man's arm to stop him before he could reach the marina, where a hundred possible hiding places awaited. He turned the man toward him, until his face was revealed in the pale blue glow of a mercury vapor lamp guarding the marina's entrance. It was the bartender, Luis.

"Real hero, aren't you, Luis?" he said as he released the man's arm.

The slender man answered in a nervous stream of Spanish. "I am sorry *señor*. I stayed behind to make sure Carly was all right. I can't get involved—you see, I have a prison record. Paolo gave me this chance to work for him."

"Who's Paolo?"

"The *jefe*. Paolo Guzman, a big man on this island. He owns the cantina, and he watches Carly like a papa."

Dan considered the man's words, which reminded him of something that had bothered him all evening. By his estimate, Carly Dawson should have a cool million in cash to watch over her. He'd expected to find her living in the lap of luxury, and found her instead in a beachfront bar frequented by fishermen and troublemakers. What did she need with a protector? Or a job, for that matter....?

"Where does she live?" he asked Luis. He could have found out on his own, but this way was fastest.

"You are trouble, *señor*. I see it in your eyes," Luis said portentously. "I cannot tell you where she lives."

The bartender nervously shuffled his feet, but didn't leave. Dan knew he had him. "Then don't look at my eyes. Look at this instead."

Dan reached for his wallet and took out several bills, stretching his palm toward Luis. Even in the faint light, the denominations were visible, and he saw the bartender's eyebrows raise at the amount.

"She lives on the beach," Luis said. "Come with me, and I will show you her cottage."

Thanks to the incident at the cantina, Carly began her morning swim a bit later than usual. After she'd locked the cantina's front door behind Dan Turner last night, she'd called Paolo to tell him what had happened. He'd joined her to help clear up and settle the day's receipts, driving her home afterward. But even with Paolo's help, it had been a long night.

At least this time she'd headed for trouble with both eyes open, she thought wryly as she dropped her towel on the sand and waded into the water. She'd made the decision to vent her frustration on the boy tormenting her, and she wasn't sorry. She'd enjoyed every moment of her little rebellion. And no harm done. Paolo was sympathetic, assuring her that if he had only been there himself, he would have tossed *los muchachos locos*—those crazy boys—out on their rumps.

She swam out to a submerged rock and back, then floated lazily, staring up at the blue sky. Normally, her thoughts drifted from the sky, a deep shade of zircon that was distinctly Mexican, to the warmth of the salty water caressing her limbs.

Paradise, some would call it. But last night, Carly was reminded once again that her life was far from idyllic. She was alone in a foreign country, and she couldn't go back home until she found another attorney who could convince the FBI that she was an innocent dupe. Unfortunately, that wasn't as easy as it sounded. Robert Daimler had seen to that.

She suspected that her stepfather was behind the resignation of the first attorney she'd hired. It was obvious that Robert was after her trust fund. Claire Cheswick-Dawson had apparently felt she was providing for Carly's future by placing the money under Robert Daimler's control until Carly had "grown up" and proven herself capable.

Carly had worked hard to gain her mother's approval, but Robert had undermined her efforts at every turn, using the friction between them to create her mother's doubts. Because of his machinations, the breach between mother and daughter had never completely healed. And now Carly believed that Robert had lied to the authorities about her activities and her relationship to Tony, putting her even deeper in trouble, and enabling him to retain control of her trust fund, which her mother still hadn't altered before her sudden death.

Carly had gone to Mexico with Tony Williamson partly to show Robert that he had no power over her. Instead, she'd handed him the perfect opening. And there was nothing she could do about it, except hope she could find another attorney willing to take her case. She dived below the surface of the water in an effort to cool her frustrated thoughts, then headed for shore, her pleasure in the day gone.

Never again would she let herself believe in a man. The only male she'd learned to trust was Paolo, who had given her a job in his bar despite the fact that she didn't have a work permit and couldn't speak more than two words of Spanish. Carly suspected he'd read about the embezzlement and flight to Mexico in the newspapers, and yet he'd kept silent. He was the only man who had ever helped her.

Until last night, when Dan Turner had entered the fray like a renegade knight in shining armor. As she picked her way across the beach, looking for seashells to add to her collection, she wondered what kind of man Dan Turner was and what had brought him to Isla Linda.

She glanced up and stopped short when she recognized the subject of her thoughts standing on the beach in front of her. She regarded him with outward calm, while inside her chest, her heart pounded like a drum. He was wearing faded jeans that clung to his muscular legs, his chest was bare and tanned, and sunlight gilded the dark blond hair that he kept out of his eyes with a twisted bandana.

Here comes trouble, was the first thought that popped into her mind. Last night, Dan Turner had been formidable, but that was nothing compared to the almost animal-like languor he displayed now as he held out the brightly patterned beach towel she'd left on the sand.

In her brief white maillot, Carly felt exposed and vulnerable. She hesitated before taking the towel, relaxing slightly when his face broke into a warm smile that reached all the way to his light green eyes. They were the same color as the bits of scoured glass she occasionally found on the beach, startlingly pale in contrast to his tanned face.

"Hello again," he said. "I thought I recognized you. You're an excellent swimmer."

"I get lots of practice," Carly said as she rubbed the towel over her boyishly short hair, her gaze not meeting his. "I live in one of those cabins."

She nodded toward the handful of tiny cottages scattered among the palms and eucalyptus about a hundred feet from the water's edge. At one time, the tiny buildings had been painted in a rainbow of bright hues, but the sun and wind had worn the wood and stucco exteriors into pale sherbet colors. A few were deserted, with boarded-over windows and gaping holes in the roofs. As his gaze went toward the empty buildings, she wished belatedly that she hadn't pointed them out.

"We'll be neighbors then," he told her.

"Neighbors? You're going to live here?" Her drying motions stilled. "I assumed you were just visiting the island."

"I am. An extended visit. I came here to get away from it all and paint." He gestured toward the edge of the trees. For the first time, she noticed the canvas set up on a wooden easel several feet away.

"You're an artist?" Carly tried to hide her surprise. Of all the possibilities in the world, she never would have pegged Dan Turner as an artist. It was far easier to picture him as a fisherman, spending his days battling the ocean like a modern-day pirate. With his dashing air and devil-may-care grin, and that unruly shock of sun-burnished hair, he certainly looked the part.

"I'm trying anyway." He grinned again, and Carly saw the wry humor in his gaze. "I'm not having much luck," he admitted. "You distracted me."

The frank words caused a shiver of awareness to run through her, and she took her time spreading her towel out on the sand before sitting down. As she stretched out her legs, she wondered why she hadn't skipped her usual sunbathing routine, said a polite goodbye, and headed straight for her lime green cottage. Even though Dan was going out of his way to be friendly, she felt uneasy in his presence. She leaned back and closed her eyes, willing him to go away and leave her alone.

She knew the exact moment he stretched out on the sand beside her. Even with her eyes closed, she was all too aware of him: his long, muscled legs, the dark golden hair that covered his chest.

"I don't suppose you give swimming lessons?"

Her eyes snapped open. He was leaning back and supporting himself on his elbows. He was also barefoot, and Carly focused on this. Somehow, the dusting of sand over his toes made him seem more boyish and approachable. She allowed her gaze to travel up to meet his and found him regarding her with a chagrined smile on his face.

"You're trying to tell me that you don't know how to swim?" Her voice was incredulous.

"Never learned."

"But everyone knows how to swim."

"I can barely dog-paddle," he told her with a rueful grin. "I grew up in a small town in eastern North Dakota—no lakes, no swimming pools. The local high school added a pool two years after I graduated," he told her. "I figured I lucked out. Now I'm not so sure. I think I'd like to swim in the ocean with you."

Carly felt as though he'd reached out and snatched her breath away. Dan Turner certainly had a knack for keeping her off balance. She hadn't had much practice at flirtatious banter. Her years of college and work had been all too serious. At the cantina, she would joke now and then with some of her customers, but as an Anglo woman she'd been afforded a measure of respect from the local men. Besides, they knew that Paolo watched over her like a solicitous older brother. The rare visitors from the States normally fell in the category of retired snowbirds or sports fishermen, and most of them kept to the other side of the island.

"How long will you be staying?" she asked, anxious to redirect the conversation onto safer territory.

"I don't know yet," he told her. "It depends on how much painting I manage to get done. I came here to prove something to myself."

"Then hadn't you better forget swimming and start working?"

He leaned back and looked up at the sky, where a solitary wisp of cloud floated lazily. "You know what they say about all work and no play." He smiled again. "How about you? Do you only work nights?"

"Yes. Six nights a week. I enjoy having the days to myself," she said.

"In other words, you don't want company right now."

Carly said nothing, torn between wanting him to leave and wishing he would stay. Spanish was a beautiful language even when peppered with the crude colloquialisms of sailors, but she was enjoying this rare chance to converse in her native tongue. Dan spoke with a midwestern twang that reminded her of her mother, who had grown up in Chicago. His speech made her think of trim green lawns and autumn leaves—harmless, cheerful things. She amended her earlier thoughts about him. Last night had called for action, and Dan had responded to the situation. Today, in a far different setting, he was as friendly and outgoing as a harmless golden retriever.

Yes, but even good dogs bite, she reminded herself as he stretched lazily beside her. She smiled at her metaphor. Dan Turner was definitely no dog. He was one of the handsomest men she'd ever met.

"That's more like it," he said. "Are you always so serious?"

"I don't have much to smile about," she told him without thinking, immediately wishing she could retract the words. She'd ended up trapped in Isla Linda because she had misjudged a man. She didn't need to complicate the situation by confiding in another. She stood and told Dan she had to be going, pretending not to notice his surprise.

"So soon? I was hoping we could get started on those swimming lessons."

She smiled despite herself. "Maybe some other time."

"I'll hold you to it," he called after Carly as she walked toward her cabin.

She couldn't resist pausing for a glimpse of the canvas set up at the edge of the sand, hoping it might give her a clue about Dan Turner's personality, and what brought him to a sleepy little island in the Sea of Cortez.

It was blank.

Dan waited until Carly was out of sight before returning to the canvas and easel he'd purchased before crossing to Baja several days ago. Her quick look at his "work" hadn't escaped him. He wondered how the hell he was going to convince her he was an artist when the first, last, and only thing he'd ever painted was his sister's kitchen cabinets.

He thought of Janie and the reason that he was here, and he decided that he'd better make it look good just in case Carly was watching him through the window of her little green cabin. He went through the motions, opening tubes of paint and rearranging the angle of the canvas. He stood behind the easel and squinted thoughtfully at the horizon, jabbing at the canvas with a brush full of paint.

After an hour that seemed more like four, he packed up and went to the pale blue cabin next to Carly's. He'd rented it that morning from Paolo, Carly's boss. He opened the door, which he hadn't bothered to lock. There was nothing inside worth stealing. And nothing to indicate who Dan Turner really was.

The cabin was one main room, sparsely furnished with a narrow bed, a recliner upholstered in a tattered brown plaid, and a small table with two rickety chairs. He crossed the uneven tile floor to the "kitchen," five feet of wall that boasted a two-burner stove, a chipped porcelain sink, and a short, squat refrigerator that rumbled like a cement mixer. He opened it now, reaching in for an orange and a hunk of cheese. He was starving, but he didn't have time for anything else. He didn't want to lose one minute in his quest to find Tony Williamson.

He balanced his meager lunch in one hand and pulled a chair over to the wide window at the front of the room. If he sat at the very edge of the window, he could see the door of Carly's cottage. Until she left, he wasn't taking his eyes away from it.

But no one came or went, not even Carly. The reflection from the setting sun was coloring the ocean pink before she finally stepped outside, dressed for work in the same short denim skirt and embroidered white blouse that she'd worn the night before. Dan waited a full fifteen minutes before walking up the path to her door. It was locked, but that wouldn't stop him for long.

Nothing was going to stop him now.

Chapter Two

Carly barely noticed the fading pink of the sky as she walked along the beach to the cantina. Her thoughts were on the events of the last twenty-four hours, not on sunsets. Meeting Dan Turner had only added to her growing frustration over the slow progress she was making toward clearing her name and reputation.

Unlike Dan Turner, who was free to come and go, to act on his wish to become an artist, to flirt with an unattached member of the opposite sex, she was in prison. A very lovely prison, to be sure, but the palms fringing the edge of the beach could just as well be iron bars.

Ten months ago, she'd been on her way to becoming an investment banker, her future assured. Today, she was a cocktail waitress trapped in a Mexican backwater, mixing margaritas and fending off unwanted advances. All it would take was a traced phone call, a tip from the Mexican authorities or from a tourist who read the papers and recognized her face, and she would be sent back to the U.S.—but not as a free woman.

She stopped and leaned against a palm trunk, squeezing her eyes shut and trying to remember what her attorney had told her would happen. She would be arrested and indicted. She could see the flashbulbs going off, the microphones shoved in her face, the sensationalized headlines about a poor little rich girl turned to crime. After a hearing, she would be remanded into custody—but not for long. Not even Robert Daimler would allow her to stay in jail. It might be bad for his real estate business to have a stepdaughter in the clink and coming to her assistance would make him look good.

But even released on her own recognizance, she would have no hope of regaining her old job, nor would she have a prayer of finding another one in her field. By the time the case finally came to trial, she would be broke, hounded by the press, and once again under Robert Daimler's control.

Poor little rich girl.

Stop it, she told herself, pushing away from the palm tree she was leaning against and continuing toward the cantina. Would it really be so bad to go back? Could she even trust what the attorney had written her? It was possible that he'd been Daimler's man from the beginning. He had asked her several times to entrust him with her location, insisting it would make communications between them easier and faster than going through her friend Jill. Thank God she hadn't told him where she was.

Maybe he'd been lying to her, part of Daimler's scheme to gain control of her inheritance. She thought of her mother, and a shaft of pain stabbed her. She didn't care about losing the trust money to her stepfather. He could have it. What mattered was losing the reputation she had been rebuilding slowly, brick by brick, since she'd become an adult.

She couldn't let that happen.

She arrived at the cantina just as the sun slipped behind the horizon. She opened the heavy wooden door and stood to allow her eyes to adjust. Even though the sky had begun to darken outside, it was darker yet in here. The cantina opened for business without ceremony at noon every day except Sunday, but no matter what time of day it was, the punched-tin chandeliers gave off no more light than candles. Paolo insisted that people drank more when it was dark.

Personally, Carly was grateful for the dim light because it helped to hide the gruesome decor. Every wall was covered with fishing trophies—marlin, tuna, and sailfish, all immortalized by a local taxidermist. She hardly noticed them anymore. Nor did she spare a glance for the scuffed linoleum floor or the wobbly, unmatched chairs.

She quickly assessed the current state of business, and saw that Lupe, Paolo's wife, was working alone, tending bar and waiting on tables where a few customers sat patiently. After running out on Carly last night, Luis had apparently decided not to show up for work. Soon, when the fishing boats returned to the marina, the crowd would be too much for Lupe to handle on her own. Carly looked at her watch and decided that if she wanted to call Jill, it had to be now. Two weeks ago, she had asked her friend, who was nearly finished with her last year of law school, to try to find another attorney willing to take Carly's case.

But before she could reach the telephone located in an alcove near the bathroom, Lupe Guzman hailed her from one of the tables.

"Carlita, *mia cara*," Lupe said, waving a plump arm to catch Carly's attention. She continued in rapid Spanish, "I almost sent one of the children to find you. We are all in a mess here. Luis told Paolo he didn't want to tend bar anymore, and we are very busy. I did not have time even to wash the glasses today."

She spun around and returned to the bar, where she immediately began filling the sink with hot water and liquid soap.

"*Pero—*" Carly began and paused. There were no buts. The phone call could wait. After all, she'd already been here on Isla Linda for ten months. A few more hours wouldn't hurt. Still, frustration dampened her spirits as she picked up a dirty tumbler Lupe had overlooked and took her place behind the bar.

Dan waited until after ten p.m. to leave for the cantina where Carly worked. By then he was starving, and he hoped the cantina's limited fare would be enough to see him through the night. He hadn't taken the time to get more than a few necessities from the small grocery down the street.

He entered the dark, smoky room and sat down at the same small table he'd claimed last night. His gaze went directly to Carly, who hadn't yet spotted him. She was smiling at a table of roughly dressed men, listening to the eldest one tell about his struggles to net a particularly large fish.

The one that got away, Dan thought as he followed the colloquial and very colorful Spanish the gray-haired man employed to tell his tale. Dan hoped his own quarry, Tony Williamson, wouldn't be as difficult to catch. He'd thoroughly searched Carly's cottage but found nothing that indicated she was living on her share of the two-million-dollar booty.

In fact, as he'd sorted through her possessions, he found himself hoping it was all a mistake, that Carly Dawson was just an average working girl who had gone on a Mexican vacation and run out of cash. From the looks of her cottage, which was larger than the one he was renting but almost as empty of furniture, she was living as austerely as a nun.

But then, in the bottom drawer of her bureau, crammed into a corner among socks and lingerie, he'd found a white handkerchief embroidered in navy blue with the initials "AW." *Anthony Williamson.* It was the connection he'd been seeking, but it didn't explain why she was living as she was. Perhaps she didn't spend much time in the cottage, he speculated. She may meet Tony somewhere else.

Here at the cantina, for instance.

He rebelled at the thought of Carly meeting Tony anywhere. Life had taught him that most people would do anything for a price, but Carly Dawson seemed different somehow. What was it about her that made him want to believe she wasn't part of Tony's schemes?

Dan searched for an answer as he watched her smile at the wrinkled old man before she returned to the bar. She was beautiful, with her bright auburn hair and luminous skin, but Dan had never lacked for the companionship of beautiful women. Carly Dawson possessed something more than beauty—a veneer of innocence and grace that was almost serene.

He nearly laughed aloud at his flight of fancy. *Veneer* was right. Carly Dawson was as capable of treachery as the next woman, and he'd better not forget it. He'd learned long ago not to trust anyone except himself. Look at what had happened to his sister for trusting Tony Williamson. And Carly Dawson was part of the reason his sister was hurting now.

At that moment Carly turned, as though she had at last sensed his presence, and looked directly toward him. Her eyes widened, and a half-dozen expressions—surprise, wariness, even pleasure—crossed her features before being replaced by a smooth mask. For a moment, he thought she intended to ignore him, but then her training as a waitress took over, and she crossed the room toward him.

His gaze was drawn to her slim bare legs, brown beneath her short denim skirt. She was wholesome and sexy at the same time, and he couldn't help his automatic response. For a brief moment, he wondered if it were possible that Tony had double-crossed her and left her here.

Don't be stupid, he told himself. Even if Tony had double-crossed her, she was still guilty of running away with another woman's husband. If Tony had dumped her, she'd gotten exactly what she deserved. And if Dan was going to get what he came to Mexico for, he'd have to quit acting like some starry-eyed kid who didn't know the score.

"Can I bring you a margarita?" she asked.

"You remembered." He'd ordered a margarita the night before, shortly before he'd done his rescue number.

"Of course. It's part of my job."

Dan held a hand over his heart and pretended to be wounded. "And here I was hoping I was unforgettable," he joked, while another part of his mind wryly acknowledged how easily flirting with her came to him. But not so easy for her, he realized, observing the becoming flush on her high cheekbones.

"Careful," she began in a warning tone. "I have a protector."

"Oh?" He fell for her opening like one of the hapless stuffed fish that decorated the walls.

"Last night he started a fight because of me. He held off two guys. Well, actually they were only a couple of scrawny frat boys, but he certainly taught them a thing or two about harassing the waitress."

"Is that right?" His smile was a bit uncertain as he realized that Carly Dawson was quicker at verbal tennis than he'd given her credit for. Out of the corner of his eye, he saw Paolo's speculative smile. Dan's landlord was mixing drinks and conversing with the men who sat along the carved wooden bar, as well as keeping an eye on his waitress. Dan decided to let Carly take this game, but he was determined to win the match.

"That's right. Besides," she told him, "not very many of our customers drink margaritas."

Dan looked around the room for verification. Carly was right. Most of the tables were occupied by men drinking beer and short glasses of clear liquid. Straight tequila, he guessed. Maybe a margarita was a gringo drink, but he needed to keep his head clear in case Tony showed up.

"Just put lots of ice in it," he told her before she left.

Dan nursed his drink for the next hour or so, his gaze never leaving Carly's trim figure. She waited on tables, mopped up spills, helped Paolo fill glasses of beer and tequila, and chatted with an elderly Anglo couple who had come in after Dan. Normally Dan got bored sitting in one spot more than a few minutes, but he didn't tire of watching Carly's warm smiles and graceful movements.

Just part of my job, he assured himself as he drained the last of his watery drink. He'd noticed that several times she went to the alcove to make a phone call, but that each time she hung up without speaking to anyone. If anything, he was as disappointed as she was when time after time the call didn't get through.

He wondered if she was trying to contact Tony. And he wished that the thought didn't bother him quite so much.

Long after midnight, Carly began counting receipts while Paolo shooed the stragglers from the cantina. At five foot six, Paolo was hardly an imposing bouncer, but his beefy arms and deep, rumbling voice made up for his lack of stature. She could hear him joking as he helped a young man, slightly unsteady on his feet after several beers, out the door. Earlier, she'd watched Paolo pocket the man's keys and call his wife to escort him home. His action probably wasn't appreciated by either the man or his wife right now, and he'd probably lose the man's business for a while, but nothing was more important to Paolo than family.

Carly liked working for Paolo, even if she didn't always like being a waitress. Through Paolo, Lupe and their five children, Carly vicariously enjoyed a normal life, catching hopeful glimpses of what her own future might hold, once she found her way out of the trouble she'd gotten herself into. A part of Paolo's extended family, she was grateful for his trust in her. He'd demonstrated that trust tonight by allowing her to close the till—a small gesture, but one that Carly appreciated.

She heard Paolo lock the front door behind the last customer as she squinted at the numbers in the ledger in front of her. She was exhausted, but she had a hunch her tiredness was more mental than physical. She'd tried several times that evening to telephone Jill, but was unable to get through. She couldn't shake a feeling of impending doom, a feeling that reminded her of the times when the entire island braced itself for an imminent storm, like the late-summer *chubascos* that could hit with the force of a hurricane.

"Time to go," Paolo said. Carly looked up, surprised that he'd spoken to her in English. She immediately saw why. Standing at Paolo's right elbow, grinning broadly, was Dan Turner.

"I'll walk you home," he told her.

The peremptory announcement prompted her to assert her independence. "That's not necessary," she said.

"Paolo agrees with me."

The two men shared a conspiratorial grin, and Carly knew it was useless to argue. Once Paolo made up his mind, it would take nothing less than a hurricane to budge him. It was clear that he approved of the younger man. While she was more cautious, Carly had to acknowledge that her exhaustion had lifted at the thought of walking home with Dan.

"I will finish this," Paolo told her, taking the pencil from her hand.

Carly relented. "It seems as though I'm outnumbered."

Paolo led them through the office behind the bar to the back exit, which locked automatically behind the two of them. There were few street lights on Isla Linda, and none at all on this side of the cantina. Dan's white shirt was ghostly pale in the moonlight.

They walked through the grove of palms that stood at the cantina's side and rear. An owl, startled by their presence, hooted eerily, and Carly muffled a nervous cry. Dan reached out and took her hand, helping her over a large spidery mass of exposed roots. His movements were confident and sure, as though he knew the grove as well as his own backyard. He didn't let go of her hand until they reached the edge of the trees. Ahead of them, the beach was a band of gray in the moonlight, separating the dark water from the dirt road that led to the cantina and the adjacent marina.

"How long have you worked for Paolo?" Dan asked as they started walking along the deserted road.

"About ten months," she answered. "Shortly after I got to the island."

"What brought you here?"

She pondered the question as they walked past the gates to the marina. Here the road narrowed, and they left it behind to walk along the beach. The damp sand was packed hard beneath their shoes. Dan stopped and bent down to pick up a piece of driftwood. She watched him toss it into the water, creating silver ripples among the darker waves. How could she answer?

Usually she told people she'd come to Isla Linda on vacation and decided to make it her home, but she realized she didn't want to prevaricate with Dan. The less she said, the better. "I came with an acquaintance," she told him at last.

"It's beautiful here. I can see why you stayed."

No, you can't, she wanted to say.

But then he would start asking more questions, things she couldn't answer yet, not until talking to another attorney. Besides, she didn't want to spoil these next few minutes. Most nights she was too tired to enjoy the view, but tonight she saw it through Dan's eyes. He was right. It *was* beautiful.

The hypnotic rhythm of the waves soothed away her earlier tension, and the moonlight turned everything to silver or black. Dan's strong features were shadowed as he looked out toward the water. Earlier, she'd guessed him to be somewhere around thirty, but the moonlight smoothed the toughness in his expression and made him look younger.

If the circumstances were different, if she were free to form an attachment with someone, this might have been a very romantic moment, Carly thought as her gaze traced Dan's profile. He looked as pensive as she felt, and she wondered if he'd come to the island because he had his own demons to conquer. After all, what did she really know about Dan Turner?

Enough to stay away, her thoughts warned.

This was the wrong time and place for a romance, and the wrong man. Someday, she promised herself, she would have it all: a career, a husband, a family like Paolo and Lupe's. During the past ten months, she'd clung to that dream the way a shipwrecked sailor clung to a life preserver.

She sighed. Dan turned toward her at the sound, and her sigh ended with an audible catch. As she looked at him, she felt that strong pull of awareness again, as though the two of them were linked somehow.

Then he smiled his devil-may-care smile, and the spell was broken.

"We'd better get you back," he said, "Or Paolo will have my hide for keeping his favorite employee out too late."

"I have a hunch Paolo would approve of anything you did," she responded dryly. "You two appeared to be getting along like long-lost friends."

Dan laughed and shook his head. "Not where you're concerned. He made it very clear that you were . . . how did he put it? Like a valuable painting that should be handled carefully and admired often."

"Paolo said that?" She wrinkled her nose and smiled. "I think something must have gotten lost in the translation. Or maybe Paolo spent the evening toasting the day's catch a bit too enthusiastically."

Dan smiled. "Paolo's cantina is quite a place. I think the tourist guides would say it has local color."

"It's too far off the beaten track for tourists," Carly told him. "No one comes to Isla Linda except to fish or to retire."

"Oh?"

Carly tensed, afraid he would ask again why she had come here. "Do you work at the cantina because you like it?" he continued.

"I work there because I need money," she returned. "But most of the time I enjoy it. Paolo lets me help with the accounting, which is similar to what I was doing when..." She stopped, shocked at what she'd almost revealed. Dan Turner had a way of asking questions that made her want to tell him everything.

"When you what?" he prompted.

"When I decided to come here," she answered carefully.

Carly couldn't shake the feeling that Dan's questions had a purpose that went beyond polite conversation. *What did she really know about Dan Turner?* she asked herself again, recalling her earlier feeling that he was better suited as a fisherman or a pirate. *Or a cop,* she realized. Or even worse, one of Tony's cohorts.

A cloud passed over the moon, and a corresponding shiver went through her as another possibility came to mind. What if Dan Turner worked for Robert Daimler? Had he come to Isla Linda to make sure she wouldn't return to the U.S. to claim her inheritance?

Quickly, she forestalled any more questions about herself by asking, "Did you get a lot of painting done this afternoon?" She increased her pace along the beach toward the cabins.

"As a matter of fact, yes," he said. "I didn't put the brush down until I left for the cantina tonight."

"Good for you," she said brightly. "My mother used to paint as a hobby. She was very good, but she wasn't very dedicated. What sort of painting do you do? Acrylics, oils? Representational or abstract?''

"Landscapes, mostly," he said after a pause. "In oil. I just dabble, really. I haven't had any formal training."

"You must be good if you can come here and devote yourself to it full-time. Do you make a living at it, or do you do something else to pay the bills?'' she probed

"We're here," he said unnecessarily as they reached the foot of the driftwood-bordered path that led to Carly's front door.

His obvious relief didn't escape her, and her suspicions grew. Apparently, Dan Turner didn't like being asked questions any more than she did. "Thanks for the escort," she said, unable to shake the feeling that their polite conversation had merely scratched the surface.

"How about that swimming lesson tomorrow?" he called after her as she started up the path.

She turned to face him. "Maybe some other time. Can you take a rain check?"

"Does it ever rain here?"

She smiled. "Just wait a few weeks until the wet season starts. You haven't seen it rain unless you've lived through a *chubasco*. Of course, you'll probably be back in the States by then."

"Probably," he said with an answering smile. "I'll see you around."

She continued walking up the path. As she unlocked her door, she heard him entering his own door only fifty feet away. She'd forgotten how close together the cabins were until now. They stood empty most of the year because Paolo preferred to direct Isla Linda's visitors to the more luxurious hotel he owned on the opposite side of the island. His renting the cabin lent authenticity to Dan's claim that he was a struggling artist.

Or had he rented it to be near her?

She glanced toward Dan's cabin in time to see him wave before he disappeared indoors. She shut her own door behind her and leaned back against it, wishing the action could keep Dan Turner safely outside the margins of her life. How could she keep fending him off when they were practically living on each other's doorsteps? When she wasn't sure she wanted to fend him off at all?

She reminded herself that her judgment where men were concerned was faulty. She had no room for a man like Dan Turner. No room for anyone. She turned on the light, and the sight of her surroundings drove home her solitary existence. One chair. A single bed. A lone coffee cup sitting beside the sink.

The lamp's soft golden glow illuminated the small front room. Over the past ten months she'd accumulated very few possessions. A small bookshelf contained her seashell collection and a couple of paperback romances lent by Edith Wright, a retiree who had befriended Carly. The narrow bed was covered with the hand-knit afghan Lupe's mother had made for Carly at Christmas. The tile floor was scattered with several brightly colored wool rugs she'd picked up at the artisans' market on the other side of the island.

Through the hallway on the other side of the room, the kitchen and dining alcove had just enough space for a small bistro table and a single chair. Carly had never invited a guest to share her table. A picture of Dan Turner, his long legs folded uncomfortably beneath the small table, came to mind. She smiled, then quickly sobered. Dan Turner would not be eating at her table. She needed to be more cautious where he was concerned, at least until she knew more about him.

The notion that he was more than an artist wouldn't leave her as she prepared for bed. What was he doing here? The question nagged at her as she picked up her hairbrush and pulled it through her short hair with impatient strokes. Lupe's oldest daughter, Maria, had cut it for her two months ago, but Carly still hadn't broken the habit of brushing it when she needed to think about something.

When she finished, she set the brush down on top of her nightstand. Dan Turner was probably exactly what he said he was—an aspiring artist. She was letting her isolation and frustration get to her, imagining all kinds of things. She opened the top drawer of the small nightstand and reached inside for the bottle of lotion she used every night to counteract the effects of the sun. It wasn't where she usually kept it. She frowned and reached around, her hand closing over it at last. She must have moved it without realizing it.

Or maybe someone else had moved it, she thought as she turned off the light. She stared into the darkness a long time before finally drifting off to sleep.

Chapter Three

Hidden in the darkness of his cabin, Dan lifted aside the shabby cotton-print curtain at his window and watched Carly's place until the lights went out. Although her shade was drawn, he could picture her in vivid detail as she moved about the room—brushing her hair with the ebony-handled brush, putting away her clothes in the wobbly chest of drawers, washing her face with the lavender-scented soap she kept in a chipped china saucer next to the sink.

Earlier that afternoon, he'd examined nearly every detail of her life. He'd even seen her nightgown, long white cotton trimmed in lace, as innocent and virginal as an angel's robe.

Was she innocent? Had he made a mistake by coming here?

Dan realized he *wanted* Carly to be innocent. That moment tonight on the beach, when she'd looked into his eyes with the moon lighting her gaze, it was as though time had stopped. He'd wanted very badly to take her in his arms and kiss her. For those brief seconds, nothing had mattered but the two of them.

Nothing. Not Tony, not the money, not even his sister's request—and that was the reason he was here. He had come looking for Tony and his partner because of Janie—Mrs. Tony Williamson. Thanks to Carly Dawson, his sister was alone with two kids to raise.

He dropped the curtain and moved away from the window, knocking over the chair he'd placed there that afternoon. It fell to the tiled floor with a clatter, banging against his shin on the way down. His curse echoed around the nearly empty room. He was a fool.

How could Carly be innocent? She was here on Isla Linda, and he'd seen with his own eyes the monogrammed handkerchief that linked her to Tony. They'd come down here together, and there was no way a low-life sleaze like Anthony Williamson would have been able to resist Carly's blue eyes and soft skin.

Dan wasn't sure he could resist them, either. And that made him realize he wasn't much different than Tony. He was pretending to be someone he wasn't, he was pulling a con...and he was falling for his target, something he had no business doing. He wasn't a professional anymore—he had resigned as sergeant of the L.A.P.D.'s bunko squad before undertaking this quest for his sister. But if he was going to beat Carly and Tony at their own game, he still had to think and act like a cop.

The last twenty-four hours had moved too quickly. He had to slow things down or risk losing everything he'd sacrificed in his hunt for Tony. He'd spent the last six months patiently following Tony's tracks, living off his savings account and occasional odd jobs while he snooped around Phoenix, called in favors from old friends on the local force or in the FBI, and talked to Carly's co-workers. The trail had led him step by step to Isla Linda. Now was no time to rush his fences.

In his seven years with the L.A.P.D., he'd learned how to con a con. The key was getting Carly to trust him, he thought as he stripped off his white shirt and let it drop to the floor. Her guilt or innocence didn't matter. Either way, she was his only link to Tony Williamson. Knowing that, he couldn't afford to get soft now.

He peeled off his jeans and stretched out on the narrow, lumpy bed. At last he relaxed his guard and allowed himself to drift into sleep. But just before sleep claimed him, he wondered why the question of Carly's innocence was so important to him. Simply because he wanted to get Tony?

Or because he wanted Carly Dawson?

Carly drifted on her back, letting the salty water soothe the tension that had been building for the past two weeks. So far, she had talked to three of the attorneys that Jill had recommended. All three had insisted upon a retainer, even after Carly explained that her bank accounts were being monitored by the FBI and that the rest of her money was in trust. She'd promised them generous fees if they would work on contingency. Two had declined. The third, a woman not much older than Carly herself, said she needed more time to think about it.

As if all that wasn't enough to elevate her blood pressure, there was Dan Turner, too. During the past two weeks he'd never been far away. When she took her morning swim, he was on the beach painting. When she was working at the cantina, he was there at his usual table nursing his usual margarita. He hadn't walked her home again, but his light was always on when she returned to her cabin, no matter how late the hour.

Just when she was sure his interest in her was suspicious, he backed off. Some days he was aloof, a polite neighbor and nothing more. Others, he was friendly and outgoing, teasing her about swimming lessons or trying to tempt her into an afternoon of beachcombing. If she was completely honest with herself, she had to admit that his interest in her was flattering—and she was just as interested in him.

She wished this time that it could be different, that she had found the right man, but her situation made her all too vulnerable—little wonder she was fascinated by the first eligible man to stay on Isla Linda long enough to become a fixture at Paolo's cantina. Dan Turner had turned her routine upside down, making it virtually impossible for her to ignore him. And he wasn't hard to look at by any means, not with that devilish grin and those heart-stopping eyes.

But looks could be deceiving, and although her instincts said he was trustworthy, she'd learned not to trust those instincts. As much as she longed to confide in him, she didn't dare.

The tension crept back, weighing her limbs so gradually that Carly didn't even notice until she began to lose her buoyancy and sink deeper into the water. Blowing out a mouthful of salty bubbles, she turned over on her stomach and swam toward shore with determined strokes. When her feet touched bottom, she stood and shook the water out of her eyes. When she opened them, she saw Dan Turner on the beach waiting for her.

She felt a dart of anticipation as she walked slowly out of the water, oblivious to the waves breaking against her calves. Even without the ocean's pull, her legs would have been unsteady. The sight of Dan Turner in denim cutoffs and nothing else would make any woman's legs weak. She felt his pull as strongly as though she were a fish on a line that he was reeling in hand over hand, and she didn't like the sense of powerlessness it gave her.

Not this time, she reminded herself. She wasn't going to let a man lead her into trouble again. It was time she found out who Dan Turner was and what he was doing on Isla Linda before she let this attraction go any farther.

"Good morning," he said. "I haven't seen you here for a couple days."

"Not for lack of trying," she said coolly, lifting her chin to look up into his inquiring green gaze. "You've been following me, haven't you?" she accused.

His glance raked her from her bare feet to her water-slick cap of hair. "Lady, in case you haven't noticed, this is a pretty small place, and we happen to live next door to each other."

"But there are other places to spend the evening besides Paolo's cantina. And other beaches besides this one."

"You're suggesting that I carry my easel and paints to another beach when there's a perfectly good one right outside my door?" He laughed shortly, and shook his head.

Carly realized how ridiculous she'd sounded and felt herself flushing. Had she been wrong about him, after all? She couldn't think of a thing to say as Dan watched her, his expression considering.

"Okay. I admit it," he said. "I've been following you. You're a beautiful woman, and whenever I look at you, I wish I knew how to paint something besides landscapes." His smile was wry as he added, "Or perhaps you'd prefer me to say something flowery, like 'my poor talent is no match for your beauty.'"

"Don't bother." She tried to hide her embarrassment with sarcasm. From his point of view, she must have sounded like the most vain, self-centered creature alive. She didn't own the beach, and he had as much claim to it as she did.

"Hey, I'm sorry that I made you uncomfortable," he said, reaching out to rest his fingers lightly beneath her chin and tilt her gaze up to meet his. She looked back at him steadily, hoping he couldn't see her instant reaction to his touch.

"The other reason I'm being such a pest," he continued, "is that I can't speak more than two or three words of Spanish, and I don't know my way around yet. You remind me of home, and you're familiar with the island. Besides," he teased, "I like your company."

He chucked her chin as though she were a five-year-old, prompting her to ask, "Even when I'm acting like a spoiled brat?" He seemed sincere, but she couldn't trust him. Not yet, anyway.

"Especially then," he said, still smiling.

Carly considered her options. She could rebuff him now and hope he would leave her alone at last. She could throw caution to the wind and pray that this time her instinct was accurate. Or she could test him, until she knew for certain just what kind of man Dan Turner really was.

"I overreacted," she said finally. "I'm used to having this place to myself. I guess I forgot how to coexist with a neighbor."

"That's okay. You can make it up to me by letting me buy you lunch. I don't feel comfortable here yet, and I'd really appreciate it if you'd show me some of the sights."

"All right."

He seemed taken aback at her ready agreement, so she added, "How can I refuse? Now you won't be able to say that the cantina is the only place you know of on the island to eat and drink."

Dan stepped out of his cutoffs and into the shower, muffling a curse as he bumped his elbow on the tile that sent a tingling numbness all the way to his fingertips. Before they left the beach, he and Carly had made arrangements to meet outside her cabin in twenty minutes. Now all he had to do was get there in one piece.

If he kept his arms in at his sides, the shower cubicle was just big enough for his six-foot-two, one-hundred-eighty-pound frame. He tried adjusting the nozzle, which emitted a weak spray that hit him in the stomach. Isla Linda was paradise enough to make him almost forget L.A. and the dregs he'd had to deal with every day. But even paradise had a serpent, and this—standing in a tiled cubicle the size of a coffin, being dribbled with tepid water of questionable purity—was Isla Linda's. He liked long, hot showers, with water pressure that felt like fingers massaging his back.

An unexpected vision of Carly rose to his mind. Right now, she was undoubtedly standing in her own tiny shower, which probably just fit her petite frame. He realized where his thoughts were headed, and turned up the tap marked F for *frio*.

The temperature of the water barely responded to the adjustment, but even all the cold water in the world wouldn't have helped. He laughed wryly. He'd faced men who'd had the boldness to pull off million-dollar scams and won. He'd dueled with cunning gamblers and beaten them at their own game. He'd tangled wits with the cleverest of cons and come out on top. But so far, a five-foot-five, blue-eyed woman was giving him more trouble than all of them put together.

He turned off the faucet and stood, letting the water run in rivulets down his body, chilling his skin as it dried. For just a moment, he allowed himself to think of what it would be like if Carly was innocent. What if this lunch could be a genuine occasion for them to learn more about each other, with no ulterior motives, no hidden agenda? An honest-to-goodness first date that might led to an evening together, a series of evenings—a night?

He'd watched her for two weeks now, hoping for a sign that Tony was still hanging around, and conversely praying that she'd ended her alliance with him. Her simple life-style bore that possibility out. But even so, she was far from innocent. During his investigation in Phoenix, he'd talked to her stepfather, Robert Daimler, and learned that Carly wasn't as angelic as those blue eyes made a man want to believe.

Angry at his weakness, he grabbed the towel hanging over the cracked commode and rubbed roughly at his skin. He dressed quickly in khaki slacks and a white cotton shirt and went outside to find Carly already waiting for him.

"Kind of slow, aren't you?" she said with a smile that turned all his good intentions upside down.

She was wearing a colorful sleeveless blouse and a short white skirt, and she looked as excited as a kid about to go to the circus. Dan felt as though he were betraying Janie, and a picture of his sister and his niece and nephew flashed across his mind.

He reminded himself again to be careful as he took her arm and led her to his car, a gray sedan still covered with dust from the miles of desert he'd driven through to get to Isla Linda. He followed Carly's directions, keeping to the coastal road until they reached the opposite side of the island.

"Here," she said, and he turned into a long palm-lined driveway that led to a soft pink stucco hotel. The two-story Spanish Colonial style building stood in the edge of the cliff like a bird perched delicately on a branch. Dan parked under the shade of a spreading acacia and followed Carly past an impressive stone fountain to the hotel's gracefully arched entrance. Above the arch, gilt letters spelled La Paloma Rosa.

The pink dove, Dan translated silently. He'd told Carly this morning that he couldn't speak Spanish, one more lie he could add to the assortment he'd told her since arriving on Isla Linda. And he knew he'd only begun. He didn't know why the hell he felt so guilty about it when she was living a lie herself.

"I never come here," Carly was saying as he reached out to open the tall glass doors. "But most of the other Anglos living on the island do."

With those casually spoken words, she had Dan's complete attention.

"Anyone I should know?" he asked, wondering if his contact in the FBI had missed the possibility that Tony had assumed a different name and was still somewhere on the island.

She shrugged her bare shoulders. "Not really," she said as they walked past a marble registration desk down a hallway decorated with a series of arches and hanging ferns. "Most of the expatriots are in their sixties and seventies and quite wealthy. They don't mix much, except with one another. This end of the island is a little community unto itself, with its own stores and restaurants. There's even a golf course. Do you play?" she asked.

"I never had the patience to learn," Dan admitted. "Isn't anyone younger? Closer to my age?" Tony was thirty-one, just a few months older than Dan. Something else they had in common, he thought distastefully.

"No," Carly answered. "But you might like the Wrights. They're definitely young at heart. Mrs. Wright paints, and they collect Mexican and Indian art." She glanced over at him. "Maybe they'll buy one of your paintings. They like to support local artists and artisans."

Great, Dan thought. *That's all I need.*

From the sounds of it, he'd definitely do well to avoid that pair. Anyone knowledgeable enough about art could blow his cover. And if the Wrights were familiar with local artists, they might possibly recognize the only completed painting in his cottage, the one he'd purchased at the artists' market just down the road from this hotel and set up on his easel to look as though it were his.

He'd let Carly think he'd never been to this part of the island. Another lie. He forced his mind from it and tried to focus on their surroundings instead. Ahead of them, at the end of the long hallway, a final arch outlined a light-filled courtyard café with the ocean and sky as a stunning backdrop. They walked through the archway, and Dan looked around him.

Crystal and silver glittered on the linen-draped tables. Conversation blended harmoniously with the watery sounds from a central stone fountain, a smaller version of the one at the hotel's entrance. As the mâitre d' led them to a table at the end of the balcony that overlooked the ocean, Dan made note of the occupants at the tables they passed. Tanned skin and brightly colored clothing gave them an air of youth and vitality that contrasted with their silver hair. Elegant jewelry peeked out from underneath tropical-print collars and adorned fingers bent with age.

"Wow," Dan said. "I had no idea there was anything like this on Isla Linda." This, at least, was true. His explorations hadn't strayed far from the square where the artists sold their work.

Carly smiled and sipped from the crystal goblet the assistant waiter had filled the moment they sat down. "Pretty amazing, isn't it? This is where I first met Paolo. He owns it."

"This?" Dan looked around him, trying to match these elegantly understated surroundings with the same Paolo who owned the cantina by the wharf and the shabby beach cottages that he and Carly rented.

"He also owns the marina," she said, "and the grocery store near the cantina. And he has a partnership in the development where the retirees live." She smiled at Dan's barely concealed amazement.

A gray-uniformed waitress brought menus, and he lowered his voice. "Paolo must own half of Isla Linda."

She nodded. "Some of the residents refer to him as *jefe*. It means boss," she translated unnecessarily for Dan, who knew exactly what it meant and what it implied.

The implications, one after another, rocked him. Who was Paolo's partner in the development? Could he be the client for whom Tony Williamson had laundered millions of dollars? And had Tony been the one to introduce Paolo to Carly? If Paolo owned this hotel as well as the cantina, why had Carly chosen to work there, rather than here?

He thought of a dozen such questions, but at the moment, the last seemed most important. "Why do you work at the cantina when you could work here at the hotel? The tips here must be pretty generous." As soon as he'd spoken he realized that she probably feared being recognized. If so, then why were they here? he wondered. Her next words provided an answer.

"This place has unhappy memories," she said, looking down at her menu. "I thought coming here today might exorcise some of them."

Her cryptic response only brought up more questions. Before he could begin to ask them, he saw that Carly had directed her attention over his shoulder. He turned to see an elderly man and woman heading for their table.

As they neared, Dan recognized them. He'd seen them occasionally at the cantina, where they stood out from the usual crowd of fishermen and laborers. Here, they fit in perfectly, dressed as they were in simple yet expensive sportswear and jewelry. The woman wore a narrow tennis bracelet, with matching diamonds that winked at her earlobes. A gold Rolex watch was strapped around her husband's wrist.

Dan inwardly cursed the interruption, but smiled politely as the tall, athletic couple approached their table.

"Carly, dear," the woman greeted, a cloud of distinctive perfume announcing her presence. "How *lovely* to see you here."

Dan stood as she joined them. She bent to embrace Carly's shoulders, her softly tinted blond curls contrasting with Carly's sleek auburn cap. Carly returned the woman's greeting, then lifted her cheek for a kiss from the husband. "Dan, I'd like you to meet Edith and Arthur Wright."

Dan immediately recognized the names of the art patrons Carly had told him about. He tried to keep his smile natural as he returned Arthur Wright's firm handshake. Not a hint of Dan's apprehension showed, but the muscles of his shoulders tensed as Carly asked the Wrights to join them.

She smiled at Dan conspiratorially as the maître d' bustled about arranging for extra chairs and place settings for the couple. Dan realized that Carly believed she was doing him a favor by introducing him to potential patrons. He nearly grimaced at the irony, quickly covering his dismay with a smile as Arthur Wright asked him how long he intended to stay on the island.

"Several weeks, I hope," he answered. "Carly tells me that you and Mrs. Wright live here," he commented, steering the conversation back to them before it could turn to his painting.

"Edith, *please*," the woman said, tapping Dan on the shoulder playfully. "I feel old enough without being reminded of it."

He smiled gamely, searching for the expected compliment. His mind went blank. Mercifully, Arthur interrupted.

"Have you tried the grilled tuna? It's very good here." Before Dan could answer, Arthur had turned to signal the maître d'. "We'd like a bottle of wine, please," he directed. "None of that domestic swill, either. Perhaps you might have a nice California white zinfandel, or a French Vouvray in the cellars somewhere, hmm?"

While Arthur and the maître d' discussed vintages and labels, Edith commandeered the conversation. She had an unsettling habit of stressing occasional words, reminding Dan of his seventh grade English teacher, and tapping on the table or his hand for added emphasis.

"Carly just told me that you're an *artist*, Dan. You *must* come join our little *salon* sometime," she invited, then lowered her voice. "Old people can become so *tiresome*. It will be wonderful to have some fresh blood at our usual gatherings."

He shuddered inwardly at Edith's choice of words. Arthur came to the rescue again, continuing as though the maître d' had been nothing more than an apparition. "Of course, shark is the most challenging catch around here, but it just doesn't have the culinary versatility that tuna does."

"Oh, *darling*," Edith scolded, "since when do you care about *eating* your fish as much as you do about *catching* them?"

Arthur patted her hand playfully before turning back to Dan. "You'll come with me the next time I take out the *Mirabella*, won't you?"

Dan barely managed a noncommittal reply before Edith started talking again. The conversation continued in that dizzying fashion over three courses. Dan looked at Carly now and then to find her biting back an amused but sympathetic smile. He winked at her, realizing with surprise that he was enjoying himself. Edith and Arthur were both witty conversationalists, and he was impressed by their vitality. It took every bit of concentration he had just to keep up with them.

When Carly refused the sauternes Arthur had ordered for dessert, opting instead for coffee and reminding them that she had to leave for work in a few hours, Dan was glad of the excuse. They took their leave, but not before Arthur had insisted on paying the tab, and had managed to get Dan to agree to a game of chess at the cantina that evening.

"Remarkable, aren't they?" Carly asked as soon as they were out of the restaurant.

"Mmm," was his neutral response.

As they crossed the courtyard with its fountain, Carly breathed in the scent of sweet acacia. She felt almost lightheaded, and not just from the wine. Sitting with Dan and the Wrights, laughing and talking over an exquisite lunch, had made it easy to forget she wasn't here by choice. It had been like the normal existence she longed for. It had been ... *fun*.

When was the last time she'd allowed herself to have fun? Carly couldn't even remember. She'd been serious about school, serious about her career, always trying to make up for her youthful mistakes.

Today, as she'd smiled at Dan across a linen-covered table, enjoying being pampered by a solicitous wait-staff, her past had seemed faraway and unimportant. Her suspicions about him seemed ridiculous now, the product of a mind too long denied relaxation and the pleasures of companionship.

"Let's not go home yet," she said as she and Dan reached the car door. "How about a walk? I always need the outdoors after I spend time with those two. They wear me out."

Dan smiled in agreement. "I hope I'm like Arthur when I'm his age," he said admiringly. "Playing tennis in the morning, deep-sea fishing in the afternoon..."

Carly heard the admiration in his voice. *"Men,"* she teased as she led the way to the cliffside path. "Always the hunters."

For a moment he was quiet, and she was afraid she'd offended him somehow. Then he laughed and reached out to help her scramble over a large boulder, and the awkward moment passed. A strong gust of wind whipped her short hair, blowing it into her eyes and scattering bright pink, petal-like bougainvillea leaves around her like confetti. She swept her hair back with one hand and looked across the blue-green water.

"It's so beautiful here on the island," she said. "Especially on this side." The hotel was built on the edge of a rocky promontory, creating a sheer drop to the sand below. The path they were on followed the edge of the cliff, descending gradually to the beach as the ground leveled out.

"Then why do you always seem so sad?" Dan asked.

She looked at him, shocked at his perception. He was standing at the top of the boulder, his blond hair tousled playfully by the wind, like her own. She was gripped by a sudden desire to tell him about everything—her youthful mistakes, Tony's treachery, her stepfather's betrayal.

She quelled the impulse, even though the afternoon with the Wrights had convinced her that Dan was exactly what he claimed to be. She was reluctant to drag him into her problems, at least not until she knew if she had any hope of leaving Mexico in the near future. Maybe then things could be different, but right now it was still too soon to trust her secrets to this man.

She looked away, afraid he might see the regret on her face as she said, "I can't talk about it."

She could hear Dan's footsteps behind her as she continued down the path. He caught up with her and grasped her above the elbow, forcing her to stop. He turned her to face him. She saw the questions in his eyes, along with a concern that made her catch her breath.

"Does Paolo have some kind of hold over you?" he asked.

It wasn't the question she was expecting. He'd managed to catch her off guard once again. "No," she said. "It's not like that at all."

"Then what is it?"

She turned, loosening his grasp easily, and walked slowly to a rocky ledge. She sat down and looked out at the ocean, which seemed to go on forever, although she knew the mainland lay about a hundred miles away. Dan sat next to her, and she could feel him waiting tensely for her answer. She sensed his strength, and knew that he would be a powerful ally. The temptation to share her burden with him was almost overwhelming.

Yet she'd only known him for a couple of weeks. She didn't know where he came from, or when he would be going back to the States. And she was afraid he wouldn't want anything to do with her once he knew she was in trouble with the law. These, and a dozen other reasons she shouldn't confide in him, crowded her mind.

She closed her eyes, willing things to be different. If only all her problems would drop away like the leaves of the bougainvillea that grew along the cliff. If only she could open her eyes and find herself on vacation, a free woman in a tropical paradise with the man of her dreams.

She felt Dan's hand brush her cheek, and dreams blended with reality. She opened her eyes slowly, and her thoughts scattered at his intent gaze. She felt his breath touch her cheek like the soft ocean breeze as he narrowed the short distance between them. As he drew closer, reality faded away.

His lips touched hers, and it was paradise. The kiss began with a softness and grew in intensity until Carly thought she couldn't bear the sweetness another moment. Discovery and wonder filled her as she returned the pressure with her lips, her tongue, every atom of her being.

Slowly she became aware of the sound of the waves crashing against the rocky cliffs below. Reality wouldn't be denied any longer. She remembered where she was, and who she was. She remembered her history of making the wrong choices, and she knew that another wrong choice could change her life forever.

She allowed her lips to linger against his cheek a few seconds more, trying to memorize the exquisite hint of roughness against her mouth. She wanted to store away even the smallest sensation, the briefest moment, so that she could remember them and relive them whenever she chose.

Then, with a small sound of regret, she pulled away.

Chapter Four

Dan's heart was racing, and he stared at Carly with surprise. That kiss wasn't supposed to happen. Her eyes were large and wet with tears and longing. He had to look away or take her in his arms again, and Lord only knew where that would lead.

He stared out over the sea, willing his heartbeat to slow down. It was only a kiss, damn it. But why had it felt like jumping off the cliff and free-falling toward the waves crashing below? Like plunging into the unknown?

Carly had felt it, too. That tiny moaning sound had given her away. Did she respond like this for every man? For Tony? The thought tore through him like a sharp knife. For the first time in years—ever since he'd walked through the police academy doors as a raw recruit—he was unsure of himself. He didn't like the feeling.

"Well, I guess we don't need to try that again."

Dan turned at Carly's words and saw a look of sophisticated amusement on her face, a look he'd bet was as false as Edith Wright's long dark eyelashes. He wanted to wipe it off and know that she felt the same way he did. He found himself saying, "Not unless there's a bed nearby."

For a brief moment, that vulnerable look came into her eyes again. Then she laughed and started back over the cliffs with the grace of a gazelle. "Last one to the car is a rotten egg," she called over her shoulder.

Dan couldn't help smiling at the childlike challenge. This was a side of Carly he hadn't seen enough of. Until today, she'd been serious and solemn. He wondered what was behind this latest burst of enthusiasm, telling himself it was vanity to believe his kiss might be behind her high spirits.

He reminded himself that he was supposed to be analyzing Tony, not Carly. That task would be a damn sight easier if he could manage to keep his mind off her for more than five seconds at a time.

"No fair," he called after her, scrambling over the cliffs to keep up. "You had a head start."

They raced across the paved parking lot. On the straightaway Dan nearly caught up. But not quite. Carly reached the car first, slapping her hand down on the hood moments before he did the same.

"I win," she huffed out triumphantly between breaths.

"So what's the price?"

"What?"

"A forfeit. Isn't that how it usually goes? I lost, you won, so you can name your price." She gave him a look that turned his knees to water. He felt the car keys slip from his hands and land with a jangling noise on the asphalt. He bent down and retrieved them before unlocking the door, glad to have a moment to compose himself. God, he was acting as goofy and awkward as a teenager.

"I'll need to think about it for a while," she said, her voice husky with laughter. He caught a glimpse of her amusement before she slipped into the seat. He took his time walking around to his side of the car, hoping to recover some of his equilibrium.

You're on a case, he reminded himself.

The reminder did little good. Carly wasn't anything like the bozos he'd handled during his years with the L.A.P.D. It would be all too easy to forget that he was dealing with a con. She could fool anyone who looked into her clear blue eyes.

"Where to?" he asked, looking straight ahead as he settled behind the wheel.

"I thought we could drive home the other way," she said, referring to the southernmost half of the circular route around the island.

"Sure," he said, his easy agreement hiding his fear that she might suggest a visit to the arts and crafts market located a couple miles south of the hotel, at the edge of the expatriot community. When Carly pointed out the colorful booths and displays as they passed, he asked evenly, "Do you want to stop?"

When she said no, he relaxed. He'd shopped here only the day before, and was bound to be recognized as the *gringo* who had paid a ridiculous amount for a pleasant seascape in oils. He realized that the island was a small place after all. The two communities might seem completely disparate, but there was bound to be some interaction between the expats and the locals. He would have to be more careful in the future.

As they drove along the deserted gravel road, she pointed out other landmarks along the way. On one side of the car, they hugged the limestone cliffs, while on the other, it was a sheer drop to the ocean below. The limestone had eroded over the centuries to form jagged shapes, and Carly named several rock formations as they passed.

"That's Mushroom Rock," she said as they neared a dome-shaped limestone projection.

"What about that?" he asked, pointing to twin mounds of sand-colored limestone. "It looks like a pair of gumdrops."

"The locals call that one Mae West Rock," she said, and he looked over to find her blushing. He caught her eye and grinned at her embarrassment. "I didn't name it," she protested.

"If you had, what would you have called it?"

She chuckled and admitted, "Mae West Rock."

After a few minutes, she fell silent. He glanced sideways and found her asleep, her body leaning against the door, her mouth parted sweetly. He slowed the car and allowed himself to look his fill. The sun and wind had put a red flush along her cheekbones and mussed her glossy hair. Her lashes were dark against her cheeks. Reluctantly, he turned his attention back to the twisting road, afraid he'd end up driving them off the cliff.

She didn't wake as he drove across the packed sand and gravel drive to the beach cottages. The late-afternoon sun made the faded colors glow and created long, skinny shadows from the palm trees. He stopped the car and watched her silently. She looked as sweet and innocent as a child.

His gaze lowered from her full lips to the soft curve of her breasts. *No, definitely not a child,* he amended. A shadowy hint of cleavage was visible above the unbuttoned neck of her blouse. Her legs were long and bare, and he found himself wondering if they would feel as silky as they looked. His imagination readily supplied a picture of them wrapped around his waist as—

Stop it, he ordered himself. He couldn't sit here another minute longer or his imagination would run wild and have them making love on the front seat of his car.

"Carly?"

She didn't wake, not even when he opened the door and walked around the car to the passenger side. He opened the door carefully, reaching out to support her when she practically tumbled into his arms. He said her name again, genuinely concerned now that she hadn't responded.

She felt small in his arms as he carried her to the unlocked cottage. He turned the knob, pushed the door open with his shoulder and set her on top of the neatly made bed. When he touched his hand to her cheek, he discovered her skin was hot and feverish. He searched until he found a washcloth and dampened it with cool water, sitting down on the bed next to her and stroking the damp cloth over her forehead until her eyelids fluttered open.

"Dan? Wha's the matter?" She giggled and closed her eyes again.

Drunk. She was drunk, he realized, a relieved smile lighting his face. He tried to remember how many glasses of wine she'd had with lunch and knew it had to be less than three. Her condition wasn't serious. He decided the best thing to do was let her sleep, checking back later to make sure she woke up in time to go to the cantina. He removed her sandals and loosened the waistband of her short skirt, exhaling slowly when he realized that his hands were trembling with the effort to keep from touching her.

For a moment, he was torn between joining her on the bed, holding her until she woke, or beating a hasty retreat while he still had the strength of mind to leave. He chose the latter.

Carly awoke slowly, confused by the late-afternoon sunlight slanting through the window and by the throbbing pressure at her temples. Then she remembered lunch. The afternoon with Dan wasn't a dream after all. The wine must have affected her more strongly than she'd realized. She'd had only two glasses, but she wasn't used to drinking. That, plus the sun and wind—and Dan's kisses—had addled her mind.

She rolled over onto her back and stared at the ceiling. Had she really kissed Dan and then flirted with him? Giggling like a teenager, teasing him like a lover. And it had felt wonderful, all free and delightful, like going barefoot for the first time in the spring or dancing in the moonlight.

She stretched and smiled up at the ceiling, idly noting a cobweb running from the overhead light fixture to the corner. As the seconds passed, her headache faded, but then she remembered the time.

She looked at her watch and sat up straight. She had to be at the cantina in an hour. She showered quickly, dressing in her usual "uniform"—a short denim skirt and a peasant-style blouse with bright embroidery circling the neckline. As she slipped on a pair of bright red canvas espadrilles, she caught another glimpse of the time, and decided she had a few moments to stop by Dan's cottage on the way to the cantina.

After all, she told herself, she hadn't thanked him for lunch. As she walked along the path of crushed seashells, she felt a thrill of nervous anticipation, blended with embarrassment. What must he think of her, falling asleep like that? And how on earth did she get from the front seat of the car to the bed?

She knocked, hoping the flush she could feel creeping over her windburned cheeks would be gone by the time he opened the door, or that he would simply think she'd gotten too much sun and wind.

But the door stayed closed. Perhaps he was sleeping, taking an afternoon siesta as she had. She debated a moment, then decided to check inside. If Dan was asleep, she could sneak away without waking him. If he wasn't home, she would leave a note.

She opened the door a crack and called his name quietly, stepping inside when it was clear the cottage was empty. Relieved and disappointed at the same time, she looked around. Dan's cottage was even more rundown than her own. Paolo had given her the best out of the cluster of six, and this one was a distant second, smaller, darker, sparsely furnished with a moth-eaten plaid sofa and a narrow cot.

She looked for a piece of paper and something to write with, and finally spotted a square notepad on a small table near the kitchen area. She started to write out her thanks, then wrinkled her nose at how young and artless the words sounded. She set the square of paper aside and started another, discarding that one, too. How could she tell him how much she'd enjoyed herself without sounding like a silly, lovesick girl?

After a few more abandoned attempts, she finally settled on the simple "Thanks for lunch—Carly." She straightened and forgot all about the unsatisfactory notes when her gaze landed on an easel draped with a sheet standing near the window. Unable to resist the temptation, she crossed the room.

Hesitating only a moment, she pulled back the sheet to reveal a skillfully executed seascape, done in a blend of blues and grays. When did Dan find the time to finish it? she wondered. For the last couple weeks he had spent most of his time with her or near her, and she didn't remember seeing him working more than two or three times.

He must have worked on it at night, or in the mornings before she awakened; the painting was too finely detailed to have been completed quickly. And yet it wasn't what she'd expected from Dan. They hadn't discussed his art very much, but she had a picture in her head of something bolder, more primitive. In short, she expected his painting style to be as masculine and vital as he was.

She was still staring at the canvas when a sound behind her made her turn. Dan was framed in the open doorway, the sun backlighting his streaked blond hair and giving his bare shoulders a burnished glow. She dropped the sheet guiltily.

"I was curious," she said. His smile was amused, and Carly could feel a heated flush creeping from the gathered neckline of her blouse up to her hairline.

"You know what they say—" He stepped into the room, and her voice joined his to finish the sentence.

"—about curiosity and the cat. I know," she admitted, shamefaced. Her explanation was hurried. "It's just that I know so little about you. I thought seeing the painting—" She stopped. "It's very good," she finished in a small voice.

She could tell by the way his eyes crinkled at the corners that he was teasing her. And yet she felt an undercurrent of tension. When he stepped close enough for her to see the open amusement on his face, she decided the tension must have been in her imagination. Unlike her, he seemed completely relaxed and at ease. He'd obviously been sunbathing. She could feel the heat radiating from his skin, and she stepped back involuntarily, nearly bumping into the canvas behind her.

"Easy there," he said, reaching out to steady her. He grinned. "I'll let you off the hook this time."

"I appreciate it," she managed to choke out. She cleared her throat. "I stopped by to say thanks for lunch." With horror she remembered the discarded notes, and her gaze went to the pile of crumpled paper on the table. He turned to see what had captured her attention.

"It's a good thing I got back when I did," he said as he turned back again to face her, the amusement in his expression even more apparent now. "It looks like you were planning to turn this place into a litter basket."

"I meant to throw those away." Embarrassment nearly overwhelmed her. She stepped toward the table, intending to get to the notes before he could intercept her. He caught her by the hand just as she reached out to sweep the pieces of paper into her pocket.

"I'll take care of them," he teased, grasping the edge of the notes and tugging.

Carly held on tighter and explained quickly, "It's just that it's been such a long time since I enjoyed myself so much that I didn't quite know how to say thank-you."

The teasing light changed to a watchful expression, and he released the notes, which she quickly stuffed into her pocket.

"You just did. Very nicely, in fact." His gaze lowered to her lips, and a brief flash of desire chased across his face.

She stepped back, bumping against the table before going to stand at the door, feeling even more like an awkward schoolgirl than she had before. "I'd better be going to work now. Thanks again," she spoke quickly before turning and practically running down the path to the beach.

His quiet laughter followed her until she was out of earshot.

Dan stood at his window and watched as Carly half ran, half walked along the beach as though pursued by the very devil. Amusement warred with desire as his gaze followed her until she was out of sight.

He turned back to the easel and pulled away the sheet that covered it, viewing the seascape dispassionately. It was a damn good thing they hadn't stopped at the crafts market today. He'd taken a chance by getting the painting there, but he had sensed Carly's curiosity about his work and knew his cover would soon be useless unless he did something to satisfy her questions. He dropped the sheet back into place and turned away, wishing he didn't have to go through with this.

Usually, he took a twisted pleasure in setting up a sting, conning a con. This time, he felt like a liar. A vision of Carly's clear blue eyes haunted him. Try as he might, he couldn't forget that longing look she'd given him earlier on the cliffs right after he'd kissed her. No woman could fake that expression of ingenuous desire. And what man could resist it?

He knew the safest and smartest thing to do would be to leave Isla Linda as quickly as he'd come, to find Tony on his own before he got tangled up in his own unholy net. But he couldn't do that, not when Janie was counting on him. No, he had to go to the cantina again tonight and hope that he'd see or hear something that would lead him to Tony. Or that Tony himself would show up to visit his old girlfriend.

The latter would be the simplest scenario of all, and the one he least wanted to see.

He pulled out the chair with the uneven legs and settled in to wait. From here, he could see the beach and the very edge of the marina. The sun lowered, creating a stunning show of colors and reflections that barely penetrated his preoccupied senses.

When twilight had fallen, he headed for the cantina. As soon as he opened the door, his gaze sought out Carly. He found her tending bar next to the new bartender, Jorge, who had started working at the cantina only a couple nights before. Jorge was a slender young ex-fisherman who had traded in his net for a steady-paying job. Only one stool stood empty at the bar, and Dan started across the room, admitting reluctantly that the lightness inside his chest was entirely due to the anticipation of being near Carly again.

Someone called his name, and he glanced toward the sound. He groaned inwardly as he recognized Arthur and Edith Wright. A chess set was laid out on the table in front of Arthur, and Dan remembered promising a game. He cast another glance in Carly's direction before making his way toward the table, trying to keep a convincing smile on his face.

"We were hoping you'd show up," Edith trilled. "Lunch was *delightful,* simply *delightful.*"

"And I'm holding you to your promise of a game," Arthur said, sweeping his hand toward the elaborately carved onyx chessmen. Dan sat down in the chair Arthur indicated, behind the white pieces. He tried to concentrate on the opening moves, but his attention kept drifting to Carly.

Carly laughing and joking with a handsome young fisherman, Carly patiently demonstrating to Jorge how to

change the beer tap over to a new keg, Carly moving from
table to table taking orders or delivering drinks.

He waited impatiently for Arthur and Edith to finish their
drinks, so that Carly would come back to their table. He
knew it wasn't right to feel this way about a mark, wanting
to be close and have a chance for a few words with her, but
he couldn't stop himself. He felt Edith's approving gaze on
him when he smiled at Carly as she walked toward their table with a tray of drinks.

"Isn't she a treasure?" Edith said loudly as Carly set a
fresh margarita next to her. "Such a pleasant attitude. And
so *lovely.*"

Dan's discomfort at Edith's obvious praise disappeared
when he saw that Carly was even more embarrassed.

"A jewel," he agreed, watching her blush with fascinated enjoyment. He snapped back to attention when he
realized he was beginning to fall for her innocent act himself.

"...and the two of you simply must join us for dinner this
weekend. Sunday night is your night off, isn't it, Carly?"

She nodded, and Dan said, "We'd love to." He smiled at
Carly's pleased expression. When she left, he watched her
walk all the way back to the bar.

Arthur cleared his throat loudly, and Dan started. "Perhaps we should make this game more interesting," Arthur
said. "One hundred dollars says I win."

Dan looked down at the board. "You've got my queen in
four more moves. That's a pretty safe bet."

"I'll give you a handicap," Arthur replied, chuckling.
"You can have your bishop back. And your rook." As Dan
considered, he added, "And I'll raise the bet to five hundred. That ought to keep your attention on the game."

At the mention of such a large amount of money, several
heads turned their way. Before Dan made his next move,
some of the cantina's patrons had abandoned their stories
of their fishing exploits to circle around the Wrights' table.

"Oh, look, Carly," Edith said gleefully, peering past Dan's shoulder to address her as she approached the table, carrying a tray loaded with glasses and bottles. "The men are in the middle of a close one."

As soon as Carly joined the circle, Dan's brain turned to mush. He watched in helpless bemusement as Arthur recaptured both rook and bishop in the next few moves, then landed his knight one move away from Dan's queen.

They were back where they'd started, only worse. *Five hundred dollars.* What in the hell possessed him to agree to Arthur's bet? *You're not on an expense account any longer, old buddy,* he reminded himself. And Arthur isn't the one you're here to trap, anyway.

The crowd around the table grew larger, and all conversation had practically ceased. Somehow Dan managed to stretch the match out, keeping his queen one move ahead of Arthur's attack, yet never letting his king go undefended. The crowd around the table became quietly animated, and Dan realized that money was changing hands among the observers as they made side bets. All of this happened in whispered Spanish.

This had to be one of the cantina's busiest nights ever, Dan thought. He sensed Carly bustling back and forth with tray after tray of drinks.

Arthur grinned. "You seem to be a bit distracted, my boy," he said as he watched Dan's gaze following Carly. His amusement disappeared when Dan moved a knight forward, taking Arthur's rook and landing three squares away from his king.

"Checkmate." Dan heard a smattering of groans mixed in with subdued cheers, and he knew at least half of the crowd was siding against Arthur. For a brief second, he thought he saw rage in Arthur's face, but it could have been a trick of the dim lighting.

"Oh, dear," Edith said, then covered her mouth with her hand at a quelling glance from her husband.

Arthur reached for his wallet and began counting out hundreds while the crowd watched avidly. "I'm afraid I'm one hundred short," Arthur said. "Would you take an IOU?"

"Keep your money," Dan told him. Seeing the stubborn pride on Arthur's face, he knew he didn't dare insult him by negating the bet. He grinned wryly and shook his head. "If I had that much cash in my pocket, I wouldn't be able to concentrate on painting. If you'll buy everyone a round, we'll call it even."

When Arthur nodded his agreement, the cantina's patrons cheered. Dan felt relieved and tired from all the excitement. He glanced at the bar to see Paolo grinning hugely at the prospect of doing even more business. He realized that meant even more work for Carly, too, then reminded himself that he wasn't her keeper.

Carly Dawson could look after herself, and he'd do well to remember it.

Carly wiped halfheartedly at yet another table. She was exhausted, even though the cantina had been unusually quiet during Arthur and Dan's match. But the less people talked, the more they drank. She'd carried enough glasses and bottles to sink a shrimp boat. Paolo had stayed to help her close and show the new bartender, Jorge, how to do the end-of-the-week cleanup. Dan had disappeared about an hour ago, leaving at the same time as Arthur and Edith Wright.

She wrung out the washrag, feeling a bit like Cinderella. She wished that Dan had stayed to walk her home, then reminded herself not to get too used to having him around. She finished up, bade Paolo and Jorge good-night, then headed for home.

Home. She was actually beginning to think of her small cottage as home. When had that happened? She rebelled against the very idea, then realized it was because of Dan

that she wasn't as anxious to leave Isla Linda as she once
had been. She wondered how she could feel this way about
a man she hardly knew. Something about him made her
want to trust him with all her secrets.

Careful, she reminded herself, but the warning wasn't as
forceful as it had been before. Tonight, she wanted to set
aside all her pressures and fears and simply enjoy the comforting quiet of the deserted beach after working so hard at
the cantina.

Her feet were sore, so she slipped off her espadrilles and
walked. Her bare toes sunk into the damp sand, and she
sighed with exquisite pleasure. The night air was soft, with
only a hint of coolness after the day's desert temperatures.
She could hear the breeze stirring the tops of the palms and
looked up to see a sky studded with stars. The walk never
failed to soothe her—except, of course, for the night when
Dan had joined her. She hadn't felt soothed at all then, more
like a downed electric wire that jumped and danced on the
ground.

And the truth was, she wouldn't mind feeling that way
again, no matter how unwise.

She heard a splash of water that was out of rhythm with
the steady beat of the surf, then Dan's voice calling her
name. She turned and searched the silvery water and found
him chest-deep, his hair slicked back.

"I thought you couldn't swim," she accused, walking
toward the water's edge.

"I can't. I'm just splashing around to cool off. Want to
join me?" He bobbed as a wave broke over his shoulders.
He managed to keep his head above water.

It sounded like fun, especially when her muscles ached
with tension from the busy night at the cantina.

"Hold on," she told him, tempted. "Give me a few minutes to run inside and get my swimsuit."

"Don't bother," he said. "I'm not wearing one. It's too dark to see anyway." She hesitated, and he chided her. "Come on, don't be so prissy."

She turned her back toward him and slipped out of her skirt and blouse, glad she was wearing a sensible cotton bra and panties and not the frilly underthings she'd brought with her to wear on her weekend vacation.

Even so, she dived quickly into the concealing waves, gasping with surprise at the unexpected coolness of the water. As she swam out toward him, she felt decidedly wicked. Not once had she gone in the water without first changing into her suit, even with the beach deserted and under the cover of darkness.

She looked up and instantly realized that Dan had disappeared. There was no sign of him on the rippling surface, and she felt a stab of alarm.

Then his face popped out of the waves about three feet away, wearing a huge grin. "Hi."

"Hi," she returned, laughing at his trick and feeling ridiculously carefree. How could Dan manage to make her forget her troubles so easily? "You seem pretty at home in the water for someone who doesn't know how to swim."

"Oh, I can tread water for a few minutes. But I can't swim more than two strokes. I sink like a rock."

"Not enough body fat," she said, her gaze running over his muscled shoulders and chest, glad the night disguised the desire in her eyes.

He stepped closer. Afraid he might see through her after all, she reacted by reaching down with scooped hands and spraying him with water. He grabbed her wrist, but she eluded him, diving under the surface.

They splashed and played like a pair of otters in the chest-deep water, their laughter swallowed by the sound of the surf. Dan trapped Carly by the ankle, and she gasped when his hand trailed up her leg. She was too weak from laughter and shocked desire to move out of the way. He surfaced only inches from her, catching her by the elbows and pulling her against him.

His mouth captured hers in a breath-stealing kiss that made her feel as though she were dissolving into the water.

She could feel the length of him, his flesh cool and water-slick against hers. She felt her legs go weak and rested her hands on his shoulders. The buoyancy of the water lifted her feet from the sandy bottom. When she floated up, he trapped her with his powerful thighs, his lips never leaving hers.

The kiss deepened, turning as wet and slick as the water that surrounded their bodies. Held tightly against Dan, Carly became aware that nothing but her bra and panties kept them from being flesh to flesh.

She gasped and tried to pull away. "You're not wearing any underwear," she said, shocked.

He laughed. "Did I tell you I was?"

She felt panicky and weak all at once. She looked up at him, unconsciously seeking his help. He released her, and she floated a safe distance away. Moonlight made him look like a marble statue, and she felt a pang of regret at losing the flesh-and-blood man who had held her in his arms only seconds before.

"How about those swimming lessons now?" he suggested.

"I don't think you need any lessons," she accused. She could hear his laughter following her as she quickly swam toward shore before she was tempted to turn back.

Lunacy. She knew now why people once believed the moon kindled crazy, unpredictable behavior. The moonlight had certainly shaken her sense of caution.

"How about tomorrow?" he called across the water as she bent to pick up her clothing. "Want to go beachcombing?"

She held her clothing protectively in front of her and turned to look at him one last time. He was waist-deep in the water, and his chest was bare and muscled. She was reminded once again of a pirate. She considered the invitation carefully, knowing that if she continued to spend time with him, the outcome was as inevitable and natural as the phases of the moon.

"Sure," she heard herself saying, as though the moonlight had indeed taken over her thoughts and actions. They agreed on a time, and she headed back to her cottage, knowing she would spend the night dreaming of pirates and statues and men who kissed like angels.

Chapter Five

Carly woke up to sunlight streaming through the large front window, the chattering of birds loud in her ears. Underneath, like a steady bass rhythm, was the sound of the surf. It was the same every morning, but today something made the sun seem brighter, the birdsong clearer, the waves more tempting. For once, she didn't feel frustration about starting another day in her paradise prison. She was filled with a sense of peace and wonder at the freshness of her surroundings. And she knew why.

She threw back the covers, glancing at the clock and realizing it was still several hours before the time she and Dan had arranged to meet. What was he doing? she wondered as she walked to the window and looked toward his cabin. She stood modestly in the shadows until she saw that the rice-straw window shade was drawn. Either he was still sleeping, or he had already gone out to paint.

A vague sense of guilt tugged at her. It seemed as though Dan hardly ever had time to paint, and today he was taking more time off to be with her. His interest in her was flattering. More than flattering—she wanted to be able to respond wholeheartedly. But she couldn't keep from wondering what would happen when they reached the point where they were both ready to carry interest forward to its logical conclusion.

She groaned and turned away from the window. What a logical, cold way to describe the act of making love. She bit her lip as she straightened the bed, feeling a bit nervous about the direction her "interest" in Dan was taking. Isla Linda was isolated, and because of that, they were thrown together all the time. And now their...relationship—she could think of no other word to describe it—was close to becoming something more. Yet there were so many questions.

How long could Dan stay before he ran out of money? For that matter, how long could she stay before her case was resolved, or before she had to continue hiding? And how could she let him get any closer without telling him about herself? she wondered as she gave the single pillow a final pat.

She made her way toward the kitchen. As she reached into her refrigerator for her morning glass of orange juice, she decided to prepare a picnic lunch. Perhaps keeping busy was the best way to keep from thinking about Dan.

But as she sliced and buttered the homemade rolls Lupe had given to her the day before, her thoughts kept returning to him. He felt so safe and steady that she couldn't help drawing toward him like a magnet. She hoped she wasn't grasping at any anchor, looking for rescue from an intolerable situation. That wouldn't be fair to Dan.

She felt a flush creep over her skin as she remembered their embrace the night before. Last night, security had been the last thing on her mind, or what was left of her mind after Dan's shattering kisses. She'd relished the sense of danger and excitement, the feeling that she was ready to soar to places she'd never seen before.

He was so open, so friendly and uncomplicated. He made her feel clean—renewed after the soul-dirtying incident with Tony. And yet what did she really know about him—except that when she was with him, her troubles seemed to drop away? He made her smile and laugh. And right now, that was good enough for her.

She put the finishing touches on a basket of food, then showered and dressed in a tangerine-colored bikini. She hesitated for a moment, wondering if the swimsuit was too revealing. She didn't have a full-length mirror, and she hoped she wasn't missing some unattractive detail, such as a hanging string or awkward tan line. She laughed at her vanity, but searched through her dresser drawers for a colorful woven scarf. She was tying it around her waist sarong-style when she heard a knock at the door.

"Come in," she called.

When Dan entered, his expression told her much more than a mirror ever could. His approving ice green gaze traveled lazily over her from head to foot, making her feel as though he'd reached out and touched her. She hid her response by going to the kitchen to retrieve the basket.

"Looks tempting," he said as he took the basket out of Carly's hands, but he barely glanced at it, leaving her to wonder if he meant the picnic lunch or her. "Shall we?" He opened the door. "I scouted ahead and found a perfect spot farther north. There's a cove with soft, fine sand and lots of seashells. And all kinds of orange flowers."

"Hummingbird Cove," she said, leading the way through the palm grove toward the sheltered beach Dan referred to.

He looked disappointed. "You've heard of it."

"I named it," she told him, smiling.

He grinned back. "Is this your private domain, or can anyone enter it?"

"Anyone can, but usually no one ventures that far from the road. Most of the people who live on this side of the island work during the day. The cove is practically deserted, except on weekends."

"Sounds like paradise," he said, the intensity of his gaze leaving her feeling a bit short of breath.

As though he had guessed that his attention made her uncomfortable, he became teasing again. He hefted the basket a few times in the air and began to complain about its weight. "What have you got in here? Pound cake? Rock candy?"

"You'll have to wait and see," she said, laughing at his joke. When they arrived at the cove, Dan set down his burden.

"Hungry yet?" he asked.

"Not really. Why don't we explore for a while first?"

They hunted for shells, chatting companionably about their surroundings. Carly occasionally pointed out a native plant or sea creature, including the orange-flowered firecracker bush that grew all along the edges of the rocky cliffs. At last, one of the cove's namesakes buzzed by to poke its long, narrow beak at the tubular orange flowers.

"Look," she said, pointing.

"I don't see anything. Oh, wait—I can see its wings buzzing."

"They're like little jewels," she said, marveling at the hummingbird's iridescent green feathers. "See the purple under its chin?"

Another one of the tiny birds swooped in, and the pair chased each other, providing an aerobatic display for Dan and Carly's enjoyment. After a few minutes, the pair flew away, disappearing with a series of high-pitched, chittering sounds. By now, the midday sun had penetrated the shadier areas of the cove, and the heat and exercise began to take their toll.

"I'm starving," Dan announced, heading back toward the picnic basket they'd stored in the shade of a leafy bush.

"You must have read my mind." Carly had packed a large tablecloth on top of the food, and Dan helped her spread it out on the sand. She reached into the basket and removed the crusty rolls, a wedge of yellow cheese, slices of ham, and rose-colored mangoes, while he watched approvingly. They ate slowly, savoring the simple meal, then lay back and watched the clouds drift slowly across the sky.

"This reminds me a little of the vacations we used to take when I was a kid," he told her. "For two weeks every summer, we'd rent a cottage on a lake in Minnesota. My sister Janie and I used to spend every minute on the beach or in the water. She and I were inseparable."

"How come you never learned to swim?" Carly asked. When he didn't answer, she rolled over onto her stomach to look at him. His expression caught at her. "Dan? What's the matter?"

He closed his eyes before answering. "When I was about four years old, I saw a speedboat hit a water-skier. The skier was knocked unconscious and nearly drowned. After that, I wouldn't go out into deep water. My father used to give me a hard time about being afraid. Finally, one day he picked me up by the shorts and threw me off the end of the dock."

She reached out to place her hand comfortingly on his arm. His flesh was cold, as though the memory still had the power to frighten him. "How old were you?" Her voice was huskier than usual, trying to imagine a child's terror.

"About six or seven."

"Oh, no. How cruel." Her eyes filled with sympathetic tears, and she blurted out, "What a brute." She shook her head. "I'm sorry. I shouldn't have said that about your father."

He turned onto his side and faced her, his eyes direct. "It's the truth. Dad had to take a lot of crap at the store where he worked, so he never let a chance go by to play the big man at home. My mother fought right back." His grin was crooked. "Our house was like a war zone, which was probably why Janie and I stuck so close."

Carly stared at him, lost for words, never dreaming someone as happy-go-lucky as Dan had known childhood trauma. He obviously didn't allow himself time for self-pity. Before she could commiserate or tell him about her own childhood, he grinned and wrapped his arm around her waist. Her indrawn breath was clearly audible above the sounds of the birds' chatter and the waves hitting the beach.

"Come closer." His look was pure invitation.

She inched a bit closer, and he sighed in exasperation and moved himself so that he was lying on his back, his head resting on her lap. He looked up desultorily and asked, "How long did you say you'd been here on Isla Linda?"

She felt a nervous jump, recognizing the perfect opening to her story. *Tell him.* The voice inside her urged her to overcome her reluctance. Dan had shared so much with her, and yet she still couldn't find the words to reveal her own secrets.

The breeze stirred a lock of his hair, and she reached down to push it way. He was so dear. Her reluctance melted away. He smiled slightly, his eyes closed, and she said his name gently. "Dan, there's something I need to tell you."

But he never heard. He was fast asleep, his mouth slightly open, tempting her to touch his lips lightly with her fingertips. He didn't stir. "I wish we could be together," she said aloud, watching his bare chest rise and fall with every breath. She rested against the trunk of a palm, knowing she couldn't sleep until she rid her mind of its burden.

She would tell him as soon as he woke up.

No, she hadn't known him long enough.

He was solid and sincere, and he'd earned her trust.

She was confusing trust with lust.

At last, she came to a decision. She would tell him when the time was right. In the meantime, she had to make very sure that it really was different this time, that she'd finally found a man worthy of her secrets. She would play it safe, take things one step at a time.

But when Dan finally opened his eyes and looked at her, his expression slumberous and sensual, all her good intentions scattered. "Did you have a good nap?" She strived for a normal tone, but the huskiness of her voice betrayed her.

"Uh-huh. C'mere." He rolled onto his back and pulled her over him with a swift move that belied his lazy demeanor.

She ended up sprawled across his chest, her hands on his shoulders, her mouth a temptingly short distance from his. Her skin tingled where it brushed the rough hair of his chest.

"I dreamed about having you in my arms, like this," he said, his gaze traveling from the swell of her breasts to her lips before returning to her eyes.

"Oh?" Her voice was a mere breath of sound, and she knew he must be able to feel her heart drumming against his hard chest.

"Oh, yes." His gaze settled on her lips. "And I was kissing you. Like this."

He proceeded to demonstrate, his mouth capturing hers in a gentle kiss, coaxing a response from her. After a few minutes of sensual exploration, he broke off, breathing hard, and she felt a sense of satisfaction at knowing he was as unsettled as she.

"And then you woke up?" she whispered.

"Huh? Oh—the dream." He smiled crookedly. "Not yet. Not until I touched you...."

He hesitated and every one of Carly's nerve endings went on alert waiting for what would happen next. "Like this," he finished. His words ended on a groan as his hands closed over her hips, bringing her even more fully in contact with his hard body.

"Oh," she gasped, fighting for breath. She gave up when his mouth took hers again. His hands kneaded her flesh, and she responded by moving her hips, shocking herself at her boldness. Dan was an adult male, a real man—not some high school boy trying to impress his friends, and not a philandering slime like Tony.

She moaned and pulled away, tears rising to her eyes because she didn't want him to think she was only playing around, a summer fling. The separation made her ache.

"Carly, what's wrong?"

He reached for her, his fingers gentle but firm as he turned her face toward his.

"We can't—I can't . . ." She started over. "There's something you don't know about me."

He froze, and his eyes were like glass. "What?"

The change in him frightened her, and she struggled for words. "I'm not—"

She was interrupted by the sound of a child's cry. It took a moment for Dan to react, but soon his gaze joined hers in the search for the source of the cry. They looked toward the beach in the direction the sound had come from.

"We'd better go see what's happening," he said, rising to his feet and holding out a hand to help her up.

She followed him to the edge of the beach, where a small brown figure hunched in the damp sand.

"It's Mateo, Paolo's youngest," Carly said as she recognized the child. She knelt and spoke in quiet Spanish, trying to soothe Mateo's tears.

"*Soy perdido,*" he said between sobs. "Teresa and I were playing by the water and she left me and I couldn't find my way back."

"*Pobrecito,*" she murmured, pulling him into a hug. She looked up at Dan. "Poor little guy, he's lost. We'd better take him back home."

He nodded. "You dry his tears while I get the picnic things together." Carly was glad of the opportunity to collect herself yet frustrated by the interruption. If only she had been able to continue telling her story to Dan. Who knew when she would find the courage to bring up the subject again?

She continued to speak quietly to Mateo, assuring him they would be home soon, holding the sturdy little body in her arms. He smelled of sea and the strong brown soap Lupe used. She rested her chin on his hair while she crooned reassurances.

When Dan rejoined them, Mateo pulled out of Carly's embrace to look up at Dan. His head tilted back as his gaze traveled up Dan's six-foot-plus length. "Carry me," he said in Spanish, holding out his arms for Dan to pick him up, and making any translation unnecessary.

"No, Mateo," Carly said.

"It's all right," Dan told her. "You take the basket. Mateo's probably heavier anyway."

She took the picnic basket and he hoisted the boy into his arms as easily as if he were a sack of groceries. He helped Mateo clamber onto his shoulders, and all traces of the boy's tears disappeared as Dan bounced him up and down, trotting ahead of Carly on the beach.

Carly felt a lump rise to her throat. Anyone looking would see a happy family scene, a mother and father on a picnic with their son. The reality was so far removed from that idyllic picture that she felt like crying.

Her momentary sadness changed to laughter as Mateo squealed in delight and grabbed a handful of Dan's hair in his chubby little fist.

"Easy there, my little man," Dan said, repeating the words in low Spanish.

The next moment, Mateo was pleading to be let down, and Dan complied, grinning as the boy raced ahead of them. He took the picnic basket from Carly's grasp.

"Sorry about that," she apologized. "I think he was so excited he forgot that you weren't a tree or a carnival ride."

"It's okay," he said. "He reminds me of my nephew."

"Your sister's child?"

He looked at her sharply, the expression on his face unreadable. "She has two, a boy and a girl. I help her out as much as I can." His gaze held hers as he added, "Her husband ran off with another woman."

"How awful," Carly said, sympathizing with Dan's sister even though she'd never met her.

Dan looked away, but not before she caught a glimpse of the anger on his face. She remembered him saying how close he and Janie were, and she felt a little envious of the unknown woman for having someone who cared for her so fiercely.

Mateo cried out again, and her envy was forgotten as she hurried to the place farther up the beach where he had stumbled and landed on his bottom. By the time she reached him, his cries were mere sniffles that dried up with only a few tender words of sympathy. In moments, he was content to walk between Carly and Dan, his chubby little legs taking two or three steps to every one of theirs as they slowly made their way toward the cluster of houses near the marina.

When they reached the Guzmans' house near the cantina, Lupe came rushing out to meet them, her arms outspread. Mateo pulled his small hand from Dan's grasp and raced for his mother, nearly stumbling again en route.

Dan's gaze went beyond the happy reunion to the house behind, and his eyes narrowed. The crudely constructed building wasn't much bigger than the cottages he and Carly rented. The cantina's former bartender, Luis, had told him Paolo was a big man on the island. He certainly didn't live like one, Dan thought as he followed Carly inside.

Lupe ushered them through a parlor where a large picture of the Virgin Mary hung above a small television set. Daughters of all sizes argued with each other, falling silent and sitting up straight as the adults passed.

"Lupe's making lemonade," Carly explained, "and I told her we would share some. It would have been rude to refuse."

"Sure," he said, hearing the troop of children fall into step behind them as they made their way to the large kitchen where a scarred wooden table held court. He let Lupe direct him to one of the sturdy pine chairs and watched as Carly greeted each of the children in turn, returning their hugs and shy smiles before introducing them to Dan.

This was the woman who had broken up his sister's family?

He shook his head in disbelief. Earlier, when he'd told Carly about the woman who'd run away with Janie's husband, she hadn't so much as blushed.

Because she's innocent, a voice inside his head insisted.

No. He refused to believe in sentimental nonsense when all the evidence pointed to the contrary. If she was innocent, why was she still here on Isla Linda? How could she be innocent, when the illegal transaction had been recorded on her very own computer, under her password? She'd left a paper trail clear enough for anyone to read.

He felt dizzy and leaned back in his chair, his hand rubbing his forehead.

"Too much sun," he heard Lupe saying in soft Spanish. "Here, drink this."

He accepted the glass gratefully, wiping his hand across the cool moisture beading the sides. Ice cubes bobbed enticingly in the cool liquid, and he smiled gratefully. Ice cubes were as rare as igloos on this side of the island. He looked across the room and spotted a modern, top-of-the-line refrigerator equipped with everything from an ice maker to an in-door water dispenser. It must have cost a mint to ship that technological marvel from the U.S. His smile grew wry as he decided that Paolo had his priorities in the right place.

"Gracias," he said automatically, before draining every last refreshing drop. He returned the empty glass and

flushed at the giggles of Lupe's two teenaged daughters. He glanced over at Carly to see her regarding him with an amused expression.

"Is my accent that bad?" he queried, belatedly remembering he wasn't supposed to speak Spanish at all.

"Your accent's fine," she said. "They've probably never seen someone inhale sixteen ounces of lemonade before."

"Oh."

Giggles surrounded him, and he overheard one daughter—Magdalena, he thought—tell the other that he was cute . . . for an Anglo.

He had to bite the insides of his mouth to keep from breaking into laughter. He shot a sideways glance toward Carly, who wore a bland expression as she thanked Lupe and stood to leave.

"I almost forgot," Lupe said in heavily accented English. "*Una carta* comes for you today. Wait here."

He could feel the change in Carly at the words. Her expression altered and she tensed as she took the envelope from Lupe's outstretched hand. A look passed between the two women, and Dan wished he could read the letter as easily as he could read their faces.

Lupe and her daughters stood in the doorway and waved as they left, Mateo poking his head out from behind their cotton skirts to stare after Dan and Carly as they started down the road that followed the beach.

Dan could tell Carly was preoccupied as they walked back to the cottages together, and he wished she would open the letter so he could watch her read it and see her reaction. Was it from Tony? he wondered.

"News from home?" he queried mildly.

"What? Oh, yes."

"Go ahead and open it."

"No, I'd rather wait until I get back to the cottage, so I can enjoy it."

"I'll see you later at the cantina, then," he said, hiding his disappointment. He'd thought she was ready to trust him, but apparently he was wrong. One moment she was melting in his arms like warm honey, and the next she was as cool as the lemonade he'd "inhaled" in Lupe's kitchen. Just when he was convinced she was incapable of deceit, all his doubts would return.

They arrived at the cottages, and Dan reached out to stay her for a moment so he could kiss her forehead. He watched her walk up the path, his gaze on the letter she clutched tightly in her hand.

Which was she? Innocent dupe—or conniving witch?

He had to know for sure before things got any more out of hand. He'd been kidding himself to think he was in control, that he was getting close to Carly just so she'd trust him with her secrets.

He wanted her secrets all right. Every last one of them.

Had she been about to spill the beans on Tony this afternoon when Mateo had interrupted? He held back a frustrated groan and headed for the shower to rinse the salty water from his skin. And to cool off, too—he was supposed to get close to Carly so she'd trust him, but he didn't know how much more closeness he could take.

Carly read the letter once more, feeling as though the bottom had dropped out of her world. The attorney who wrote it advised her to return to the States immediately and face charges. If Carly would do that, she would take the case on a contingency fee basis. She warned Carly that continuing to hide suggested guilt. Public trial was the only way to clear her name, she insisted. The idea sent a chill of fear over Carly, but what alternative did she have?

Carly turned the envelope over and glanced at the postmark. It was mailed over a week ago. She closed her eyes and longed for the telephone she'd once taken for granted, along with her silver phone card. That and all her other credit cards were stashed away in a corner of the desk in the cantina's back office, waiting for the day she might be able to use them again. Even Paolo didn't know about them.

She considered her alternatives. She couldn't stay on Isla Linda forever, always longing for a normal life. And now that she'd met Dan, she wanted that life more than ever. If not with him, then with someone else.

Who was she fooling? It was Dan she wanted. She was in love with him, even more after his confessions today about his unhappy childhood. She wanted his loyalty, his strength. Her stepfather, Robert Daimler, wouldn't stand a chance, she thought as she remembered the first night she met Dan and how easily he had discouraged the young men bothering her.

If she could have Dan at her side, she'd be willing to face the ordeal of a publicity-filled trial and even take the risk that she'd be convicted. If that happened, of course, she would play right into her stepfather's hands. But it wouldn't happen, not with Dan to stand beside her.

Her pleasant imaginings ended. She knew that Dan would give her the support she needed, but it wasn't fair to involve him, especially if he returned her feelings. He deserved a woman who was free to love him. She stared out the window until the sun lowered, moving only to shower and dress for work. Tonight the routine seemed even more oppressive than usual.

Somewhere between the cottage and the marina, Carly decided that before she did anything about the letter and the attorney's offer, she would talk to Dan and seek his advice. But first, she had to wait for the right moment to tell him about her past.

As he'd done only days ago, Dan waited for Carly to leave, then went to her cottage. He stepped inside the door, unlocked this time, and hesitated. The tidy, sparsely furnished interior didn't seem as impersonal as before, and he couldn't be as objective as he sorted through her things looking for the letter. He kept linking her possessions with what he'd learned about Carly—a tiny bottle of perfume with the scent of her skin, a childishly drawn picture with her tenderness for Mateo.

When his hands lingered on the orange swimsuit she'd worn the day before, he told himself he was being ridiculous. He shoved the scanty pieces of cloth aside and continued his search through the chest of drawers. When he found the envelope stuck in a corner of the bottom drawer, his heart soared and sank at the same moment. At least it wasn't from Tony. He stared at the U.S. postmark with relief. But the stationery letterhead had been torn away, and without it, there was no way he could identify the sender.

He wondered if the letter had been sent this way, or if Carly had removed the letterhead in order to keep the sender's identity secret. If so, she must be guilty. The gesture was condemning in itself, and he hadn't even read the letter yet. He held it in his hand, wishing that he could hear the words from her own lips instead.

Reluctantly he read:

Jill has explained your situation, and I am willing to take your case if you come forward by returning to the U.S. It will be a tough fight, but running from it only confirms your guilt in the eyes of the authorities. If you trust the law and hope Tony will be found, your chances of acquittal are high.

Dan read it twice more, hoping each time it would say more than it had before. But no matter how many times he reread it, nothing in the letter provided conclusive proof. Nor did the letter begin to address his personal concerns. Did Carly know Tony was married? Could any woman be that innocent, that naive?

He closed his eyes, and thought of her blushes, her shocked awareness of him. Wasn't that all the proof he needed? Or was he letting his feelings for her cloud his judgment?

And now he had to make a choice—his sister or Carly.

He knew he had to go to the cantina again and watch her, waiting for a sign she was still in contact with Tony, even though he'd rather go to his own execution. And he knew he'd feel like dying if Carly was still involved with the man who had betrayed his sister.

Chapter Six

"*Perdoneme*—Sorry," Carly said for what seemed like the hundredth time as she slopped beer over the edge of a glass and onto one of the cantina's scarred tables, missing a customer by inches. She vowed to try harder to keep her mind on what she was doing, but all she could think of was the letter. The attorney's advice only added to the pressure she felt. She'd torn off the edge of the stationery with the woman's name and phone number and put it in her skirt pocket so it would be handy whenever she was ready to make the fateful phone call.

Out of the corner of her eye she saw Dan enter and make his way toward the telephone. *Great*, she thought sourly as she returned to the bar, *another distraction*. Just what she needed. Jorge clicked his tongue when she told him to make a margarita. She glanced down at the young bartender's hands and saw that he'd already started mixing Dan's usual drink, with lots of ice, the way Dan always ordered it.

"I'll take it to him this trip," she said, forgetting to speak in Spanish. She repeated herself so that Jorge could understand, ignoring his teasing grin as he added the drink to her tray of beers.

Dan was heading for a table as she delivered the round of beer to a group of fishermen. When she set the drink at Dan's elbow, he looked up in surprise.

"Be careful," she warned. "You're becoming predictable."

"I hope not," he said, but the teasing words rang flat and, even in the dimly lit cantina, she could see that his grin didn't quite reach his eyes. Accustomed to the full force of his smile, she guessed right away that something wasn't right.

"Is anything the matter?" she inquired.

"No, everything's fine," he told her, but she felt a flicker of alarm at his serious expression. "I think you'd better take care of your other customers," he told her, looking pointedly at a neighboring table, where one of the occupants was gesturing impatiently for service with a raised, empty glass.

She held back a frustrated groan, wishing she and Dan could share a quiet moment together to talk. She could find out what was bothering him, and once they'd broken the ice, telling him her own troubles would seem less awkward. She glanced at her watch as she waited for Jorge to fill more glasses, willing the time to pass quickly so she and Dan could be alone, and she could get her confession over with.

Awkward. What a mild word to describe the mess she was in. She shoved aside her feelings of doom and tried to act lighthearted as she circulated between the tables and the bar, greeting those she knew and hoping she managed to fool everyone.

She succeeded too well, she decided as she tried to discourage an enthusiastic and slightly drunk young fisherman from La Paz who was spending the evening on the island. "I'll be sure to return soon," he said, his Spanish liquid and romantic, his eyes dark with promise. Carly glanced at Dan to find him glaring. The young man's gaze followed hers like a line to Dan's shark-like, cold anger. The young Mexican quickly dropped his suit.

Dan's protectiveness made her smile. Dan would be a good man to have on her side—if he still wanted anything to do with her after he heard her tale.

Dan watched Carly, wishing he could regain his professional objectivity. The phone call he'd made to Smithy hadn't gone well at all. Smithy had nothing to say that Dan wanted to hear, and they'd nearly started to argue over the phone lines. Now the last shreds of his professionalism were being torn away as he watched Carly with the young would-be Romeo. He wanted to mash the kid's handsome face in.

"Well, well," a familiar voice drawled. "Looks like this might be a good time to win back my money."

Dan turned, grinning sheepishly as Arthur and Edith Wright joined him at the table. His grin faded when he saw that Arthur wasn't joking. He carried a chess set, and signaled for Carly to bring drinks. With a sense of resignation, Dan helped him set up the pieces. No doubt Arthur would win—Dan couldn't keep his mind on anything but Carly.

He'd hoped the FBI would see his side of things, but the most Smithy had to offer was a lukewarm "We'll see." Unfortunately, Monday was the earliest he could arrange a meeting with Smithy. Until then, his friend had warned, *stay close to her. You never know when she might meet Tony.* Smithy had nixed Dan's suggestion that he come clean with Carly and convince her to help them find Tony in exchange for immunity.

No deals, Smithy had said. In the meantime, Dan knew, he'd be suffering, staying close without going over the edge.

Carly smiled at him when she returned to the table with Arthur and Edith's order, and he felt like a rat for keeping anything from her. The game seemed to stretch out for an unbearably long time, proceeding as Dan had feared, with

Arthur gleefully announcing "Checkmate," only a few minutes before the bar closed.

"I think that makes us even," Arthur told him. "Want to play again? For money this time?" he added in a whisper as Edith's attention was momentarily distracted.

"No, thanks. It's late," Dan pointed out.

"Perhaps tomorrow night, then?"

"Oh, no, dear, don't you remember?" Edith broke in, her attention caught at last. "Carly and Dan are having dinner with us tomorrow night. It would be rude of you men to play a silly game and leave us poor ladies to entertain ourselves."

Dan felt like an animal watching the jaws of a trap closing in. The last thing he wanted to do was spend Sunday night with the Wrights. Sunday night was his final opportunity to pretend Carly was innocent, to fool himself into thinking that there might be a chance for them. Monday he had to meet Smithy and find out how the FBI wanted him to proceed if Tony didn't happen to show up. He thought distastefully of some of the methods of pursuit and persuasion he'd used as a cop in order to get at the truth.

Ah, hell, he thought morosely. He wanted the next twenty-four hours alone with her, but he didn't want to learn the truth. In his case, ignorance was bliss. As long as she didn't speak Tony's name, he could go on living this fantasy existence of sea and moonlight and kisses on the beach. A tropical paradise, complete with a beautiful woman.

He heard conversation going on around him, even managed to respond in all the right places, charming Edith without even trying. He guessed Arthur paid more attention to boats and games than to his wife. Right now, for instance, he was caught up in a game of liar's dice with Paolo, who'd arrived moments ago to help close up the cantina for the night.

Now that was an interesting choice of game for Paolo Guzman to be playing, he thought.

Edith mentioned Carly's name, and Dan's attention snapped back to the conversation at hand. "She is lovely, of course, but sometimes she seems so sad. Like tonight. I think she's here running from a broken heart," Edith confided in a dramatic whisper.

Dan felt a stab of anger as he thought of Carly being brokenhearted over a slimeball like Tony. Could Tony have used her, too, the way he'd used Janie? Lied to her, cheated her? Dan simply didn't know anymore. His whole framework of reality had been turned upside down, maybe because he was starting to believe in this role he was playing.

He had to get out, get some fresh air. He pushed back his chair. "I have to leave," he told Edith. "I want to start painting early in the morning while the light's good." He was only half-surprised at how easily the deception came to his lips.

He shouldered his way through the crowd to where Carly was standing at the bar, laughing with Jorge and keeping an eye on the game between Arthur and Paolo. The bartender quickly retreated at Dan's purposeful glance.

"Hi," Carly said with a melancholy smile. Edith was right—Carly did have an air of sadness sometimes. Like now, for instance. He wanted to erase it. In fact, he wanted to erase everything that made them who they were. Without the past, they could be together, just two people with the sea and the moonlight. He thrust away the tempting dream.

"I'm going home," he told her.

Her expression changed to alarm, and he realized she was reacting to his choice of words.

"Back to the cottage," he corrected.

"Oh." She laughed, her relief obvious. "For a moment I thought you were going back to the States."

"Not without you," he said quietly, watching her expression.

Her eyes looked huge in her face, and he could see the rapid rise and fall of her chest underneath her blouse.

Someone bumped into him from behind, and the jarring movement broke the spell. The drunk slurred an apology before ordering *una mas cerveza*.

"No more beer," Carly told him in clearly spoken Spanish. "We're ready to close." She turned back to Dan, her expression wry. "I'll be through here in less than an hour. Will you still be awake?"

Understanding came with a rush of heat that caught Dan by surprise. He wondered if she knew what she was suggesting. "Yes," he heard himself say automatically. "I'll be waiting for you."

He shouldn't have told her he'd be waiting, he thought as he walked along the beach. He wanted everything Carly was ready to give him, and yet he knew he couldn't take a thing. He had some principles left, by God. His blood burned, nearly making him a liar.

The air was muggy, no relief at all. When he got to the cottage, he couldn't settle down enough to sleep. A swim might help to clear his senses, he decided. He exchanged his jeans for cutoffs, wondering why he wanted to preserve Carly's modesty now, when only a few days before, he'd swum in the nude with her.

Maybe he wanted her to undress him. The thought popped into his mind unbidden, and the image of her hands touching him made him instantly aroused. He ran across the beach, heedless of the sharp rocks mixed in with the sand, and jumped into the water. Cool waves eased his need.

After a few minutes he climbed out and lay back on the sand, staring up at the star-studded sky. In L.A. you could barely see the stars, but here even the Milky Way was visible, a band of bright light that stretched across the sky.

He didn't even realize he'd fallen asleep until Carly woke him. He opened his eyes to see her sitting beside him on the sand, dressed in her orange bikini. "I wasn't sure whether

to wake you or not. You looked like a merman," she teased.
"I thought I might be dreaming."

"Aren't we?" He rolled over onto his stomach, his gaze
capturing hers as his hand reached for her ankle.

It closed over nothing but air when she jumped up and
headed for the water's edge. "How about those swimming
lessons?" she called over her shoulder as she waded into the
water.

He smiled, wondering at her skittishness. "It's the middle of the night. How am I supposed to swim if I can't see?"
But she was already underwater. When she didn't reappear
for several moments, he rushed out, his heart beating wildly.

"Carly, where are you?"

He jumped as a wet hand grasped his thigh underwater.
"Right here," she said, surfacing and grinning up at him.
Her face cascaded with water, and her hair was slicked back,
giving her features a new vulnerability. "I owe you one, remember?"

"You scared me," he said. "You shouldn't clown around
like that when you know I couldn't help you if something
happened."

"Then I guess you'd better learn to swim so you can rescue me next time," she teased, floating out of his reach. He
stepped toward her and got a mouthful of water when he
realized it was deeper than he expected, nearly over his head.

"Are you ready?" she asked.

He was nervous about displaying his weakness around
her, but he wanted the night to last as long as possible.
Thirty-six more hours until meeting Smithy, he reminded
himself. "Sure," he said, his voice husky. "I'm in your
hands."

"Then trust me and let yourself float toward me."

Trust her? God, he wanted to. But most of all he wanted
to trust himself, he realized as he felt his feet lose solid bottom. Mistrust had been ingrained in him, from the time he
was a child watching his parents stab at each other to his

years as a cop. Was it too late to learn how to trust? He followed Carly's instructions and let himself float freely.

"You're doing great," Carly told Dan, feeling as though she had to push her voice out of her chest.

It was increasingly difficult to touch him and pretend she was merely showing him the proper stroke or helping to support his weight. They had been out here in the moonlight forever, it seemed. His skin was slick, and he kept sliding against her bare midriff, sending shock waves through her that were even stronger than the pull of the surf.

He swam away from her, and she regained her equilibrium enough to tease, "You're not sinking. Maybe you've put on some fat since the last time you tried swimming."

She squealed with surprise as Dan quickly changed direction and splashed her. Laughing, she swam out of reach, heading for a partially submerged rock several yards away.

"Hey, no fair," Dan called after her.

"Come on," she challenged. "You can make it." She watched him slice through the water, his form only slightly choppy. He'd been a fast learner, not afraid of the water, although it was difficult at first to get him to relax. He'd jumped a foot every time she had touched him.

Not a problem now, she thought, as he pulled himself up beside her onto the rock's flat surface. He grinned. "I did it."

She smiled at his obvious satisfaction. "I think you've got the hang of it."

They lay back side by side, staring up at the stars, the only two people in the world, or at least it seemed that way for now. The sound of the waves was as lulling as the knowledge that the rest of the island was asleep. But Carly's enjoyment was marred when thoughts of the letter returned. She had to tell Dan about her situation.

She heard him sigh. "If I could do this every day," he said, "I'd be a happy man."

She wondered why he wasn't happy all the time, and that caused her to ask carefully, "Do you think we can overcome our pasts?"

He rolled over onto his stomach and looked at Carly. "What do you mean?"

The lines and angles of his face looked more tense than usual, or perhaps it was a trick of the moonlight and Carly's apprehensive imagination. Nervously, she began, "Earlier today you talked about your childhood. You seem to have overcome the fact that you grew up in such an angry household."

"Sometimes it feels like an act," he admitted. "It took me awhile to work things out. I had problems in school."

"I did, too," she confessed. Her words were lost in the sound of the waves, and talking to him became easier. It was just the two of them, after all, and she knew Dan would keep her secrets. "Did you ever talk to anyone about it? Your teachers, maybe?"

"No, only Janie, my sister."

"I wish I'd had a sister to talk to. My mother..." She hesitated. "My mother didn't want to hear." She swallowed. She hadn't meant to mention this part of her past at all, but the words seemed to pop up on their own. What did it have to do with anything?

"What happened?"

Now that she'd had a moment for second thoughts, she wished Dan might have dropped the subject. However, she could tell by the curiosity in his gaze that he wasn't about to give up. She swallowed and began speaking in a low voice. "Once, my stepfather came into my room late at night. He tried to—" The words caught in her throat. "He touched me. I was twelve years old and petrified. I threatened to tell Mother, and he laughed at me. When I started screaming, he left. I told my mother I'd screamed because I'd had a bad dream," she finished, her voice shaking.

Dan watched her, his eyes gentle. "You never talked to her about it?"

"I couldn't. She loved him, you see. He was her fourth husband, and she thought that this time she'd found someone who cared about her more than her money." She tried to laugh, but the sound stuck in her throat. "Robert told me it was my fault, and he used what happened as a threat. It was a way of controlling me. I understand that now, but then I was too young and scared."

"Poor little rich girl," he said quietly, not at all in the disparaging way she'd heard from her classmates or anyone she'd tried talking to before. His voice was tender, and when he took her into his arms, she felt sheltered and protected. She remembered why she'd come out tonight, to tell him about Tony, but after talking about the ugly incident with her stepfather, she felt drained.

She snuggled closer against his chest, and felt the stirring of desire. She still wanted to make love to Dan, but she knew it wouldn't be right until she told him everything. She didn't move, but he must have felt her withdrawal.

"It's late," he said. "Let's head back into shore."

She felt a swell of gratitude at his understanding. He was so gentle and strong, giving her the time she needed. It was different this time, she decided. This man was worthy of love, a man she could trust with her very soul.

They swam back to shore side by side, and Carly was pleased to note that Dan was able to hold his own against her more practiced strokes. He walked her to her cottage and held her close for a few moments before kissing her lightly.

"I guess this night had to end sometime."

"It doesn't have to end now," she said quietly, raising her gaze to meet his, knowing that she could find the strength somewhere to talk about Tony if it meant being able to spend the night in Dan's arms.

His eyes filled with desire, and she could see him struggling with himself before answering. His hands tightened briefly on her shoulders as he gently refused her unspoken invitation. "I think we'd better say good-night."

He kissed her on the forehead before walking to his cottage.

Dan felt his whole perspective shifting, like the sand at his feet as he walked along the water's edge. The early-morning sun beat down on his bare shoulders, and he was glad to be out of the moonlight and the madness that seemed to go along with it.

He'd hardly slept a wink after saying good-night to Carly just hours ago. He still felt passion for her, and that didn't surprise him. Carly was a beautiful, desirable woman. But even more so after last night, he'd felt an ever-growing desire to keep her safe from men like Tony. *Or Smithy.*

This protectiveness frightened him. It changed him. He could have taken her last night. He recoiled at the crudeness of the words, reaching down to pick up a small rock and fling it far out to sea, wishing he could get rid of these unwanted feelings as easily. Last night, he could have played out the fantasy, holding her tightly, hoping that the moonlight would last forever and that Monday would never come.

But Carly wasn't some dream girl, she was a flesh-and-blood woman who'd been badly hurt by the men in her life, according to the case file the FBI had given him to read. And she was about to be hurt by one more. Now that everything seemed gray, the black-and-white simplicity of the law taunted him. He wasn't a cop any more. What's more, he realized, he didn't want to be. He faced a chasm of uncertainty as he tried to determine what was going to happen after he turned Carly over to the U.S. authorities.

He stared out at the azure water without seeing it. What would his life be without police work? It was all he knew—he sure as hell couldn't paint. What on earth was he thinking, wishing that he and Carly could hide out here forever? The idea tempted him more than he could admit. They were

just two weak people, some guy who couldn't bring himself
to do his job, and a woman who fell for every guy who came
along.

He sank onto the sand, sitting with his hands on his
knees. Whenever he thought of his sister, he knew he
couldn't trade his responsibilities for some half-baked, impossible fantasy. Smithy's words came back to haunt him:
Stay close and watch her.

He'd do as he was told. He'd take her to the Wrights' tonight and smile like a fool through all of Edith's match-
making attempts. But if he found out Carly was still
involved with Tony, he knew the truth would destroy him.

Carly's closet didn't yield much in the way of evening
clothes. She'd brought one "little black dress" for her
weekend with Tony. It seemed like aeons since she'd purchased it on a lunch-hour shopping spree to the mall in
downtown Phoenix. She looked at the elegant dress with
distaste, then pulled it off the hanger, knowing it was her
only reasonable option.

She slid the dress on, pleasantly surprised by her reflection in the hand mirror. She looked slim and fit. She turned
and adjusted the mirror in order to reveal her full length,
one small area at a time. The dress had cutaway shoulders,
making a bra impossible. She didn't need panty hose, and
it was too hot to wear the long-sleeved bolero jacket. But her
skin was smooth and tanned, the muscles in her arms more
defined than they'd ever been.

She used some blush and shadow from the travel bag of
makeup she'd hoarded over the last few months. Normally,
she wore nothing more than lip gloss, but tonight she wanted
to look more confident than she felt. She'd hardly seen Dan
all day, and she was a bit nervous about going with him to
the Wrights'—especially since she'd decided to tell him
about her situation as soon as the ordeal with Arthur and
Edith was behind them.

Dan's heated glance when he met her at the door gave her all the confidence she needed. He was wearing dark slacks and a white shirt, with a tie—an item of clothing she'd never seen him wear. He looked uncomfortable, an impression he confirmed by reaching up to pull at the tight knot on their way to the car. As they drove along the road to the other side of the island, the sun was setting, turning the rocky cliffs orangy-gold.

The Wrights' house was in the heart of the planned and landscaped expatriot community. A long palm-lined driveway led to a sprawling stucco-and-glass structure with overhanging decks and pilings that made it look as though it were balancing on the very edge of the cliffs. A string of fairy lights welcomed them up the long flagstone walkway.

Dan's low whistle reminded Carly that not everyone had grown up in this kind of environment. When she saw the house through his eyes, she realized that the Wrights were very wealthy people.

Edith opened the wide, carved double doors before they had a chance to use the cast bronze knocker. She hugged them both in greeting before pulling them inside the grand foyer, talking constantly, reminding Carly of a noisy parrot in her bright emerald silk pantsuit. As they passed through the tiled hallway, Carly noted the artifacts and artwork arranged in niches with subtle recessed lighting. She'd seen them all before on her previous visits to the Wrights' home, but she'd never mentally added up their worth the way she was doing now. She glanced at Dan and saw that he, too, was examining his surroundings with a critical eye. Of course, as an artist, he would be particularly interested in Arthur and Edith's extensive collection.

Arthur met them at the arching doorway to the living room. When he noticed Dan's interest, his enthusiasm took over, and he became like a little boy showing off his treasures, leading Dan from one vase or statue to the next, while

Edith fussed over the platter of appetizers arranged on an antique table in the living room.

"Conchita made crab-and-shrimp appetizers. Won't you try one? Arthur dear," she called, "do stop monopolizing Dan and find us another bottle of wine. This one is almost finished."

Arthur disappeared to the wine cellar, while Edith shook her head over the appetizers. "These are far too salty. I must have a talk with Conchita. Excuse me for a moment, please."

Edith wandered toward the kitchen, leaving Dan and Carly standing by themselves in the large open room. He turned to her and asked, "What did you say Arthur and Edith did before they retired to Isla Linda?"

"They were both college professors. Anthropology or archaeology, I think. At least that would explain their interest in collecting artifacts."

"Some of these things should be in a museum, Carly." He turned and looked around at the paintings, furniture, and other valuable antiques and works of art.

"I guess so," she said slowly. "I never really thought about it before."

"I suppose you're used to living like this," he said, shaking his head.

"I'm not now," she pointed out quickly, wondering why her moneyed background seemed to bother him all of a sudden.

They wandered over toward the seating area, where a trio of white leather sofas were clustered beneath a dramatically large seascape done in blues and grays. Before she could sit down, Dan led her away to look at a small figurine across the room.

"Let's go this way," he suggested after they'd finished admiring the figurine, leading the way through the tall arch into the hall.

Carly followed, smiling at Dan's curiosity about the Wrights' home. Their footsteps echoed on the hand-painted tile. They paused at an alcove that appeared to be a photo gallery, casual compared to the displays throughout the more public areas of the house. Carly had never been in this section of Arthur and Edith's home before, and she was about to suggest to Dan that they return to the living area when her gaze was drawn to a small, framed snapshot.

Her fingers went numb, and she nearly dropped her wineglass as she stared at a photograph of Arthur Wright and another man, holding up a gigantic sailfish between them, grinning triumphantly toward the camera. Her breath squeezed out of her chest in a painful gasp.

The other man was Tony Williamson.

Chapter Seven

"There you are." Arthur's voice cut through Carly's shock. "We thought you must have gotten lost."

Carly instantly tried to compose her features, acutely aware of Arthur's steady regard. "We were just looking at your photographs," she said, her smile feeling strained and unnatural. She could feel Dan's sharp gaze on her.

"Oh, these are nothing—just family and acquaintances. Why don't you come with me back to the east wing? I have an Ansel Adams that I'd like to show you."

He gestured with a sweep of his arm and Carly walked ahead, her legs unsteady. Somehow she made it to the east wing dining area, kept up her side of the conversation, ate, and even complimented the dishes set before her, all the while wondering what a photograph of Tony Williamson was doing in Arthur and Edith's home.

Tony had come to Isla Linda because he had connections here, and in such a small place, he and Arthur were bound to run into each other at some point. Had he managed to hide his true nature from the Wrights as he had from her? Or was she wrong about Arthur and Edith, too?

She didn't recall taking a second helping of the Lobster Newburg and, her appetite gone, she stared at her full plate helplessly while conversation buzzed around her. Cold water was about all she could manage, and she drained her glass several times. When she heard Dan ask Arthur about deep-sea fishing, her hand stilled on the cut-crystal goblet. The subject revived the photograph of Tony in her mind.

"I have a sixty-five-footer that I take out two or three times a year," Arthur was saying.

"We make a party of it," Edith chimed in. "We invite several couples and stay out two or three days."

"Sounds like fun," she heard Dan say.

"It is. We have a marvelous time. Arthur—" Edith turned to her husband, her expression delighted "—why don't we take Dan and Carly next time?"

Arthur looked surprised at Edith's suggestion but quickly recovered his joviality. "Of course. Wonderful idea. It isn't the best time of year right now, with the rainy season coming up and all, but I'll see if I can organize an outing while Dan's here." He turned to Dan. "How much longer will you be staying with us? I don't believe you ever said specifically."

Before Dan could answer, Arthur's attention was distracted by Conchita's entrance, and the untimely interruption nearly made Carly groan aloud.

"Thank you, Conchita," Arthur said as the maid cleared their plates.

Carly held her breath, hoping Arthur would continue the conversation. When he turned his white head back to Dan, his expression inquiring, she exhaled in relief.

"I'm not sure," Dan replied, toying with his knife. "A few more weeks, maybe."

"Then we have plenty of time to plan something. Do remember to bring more water for Carly this time, Conchita," Arthur said to the petite, dark-haired maid.

Carly would have felt sorry for Conchita, but her mind was on Dan's noncommittal reply. *A few more weeks*. The topic switched, and Carly's thoughts wandered back to Tony and the Wrights.

She'd certainly misjudged these people, and she wondered once again if she should trust her instincts anymore. If she'd been wrong about Arthur and Edith, what about Dan? When he had first arrived on Isla Linda, she hadn't trusted him. She shoved the doubts aside, knowing she needed to trust someone or go crazy. And she wanted to trust Dan.

Dan watched Carly the rest of the evening as they lingered over dessert in Arthur and Edith's magnificent formal dining room, with its wide bay overlooking the Sea of Cortez. Even at night the view was spectacular—the darker silhouette of the cliffs was visible against the indigo sky, the lights from La Paloma, the hotel, twinkling along the rocky outline.

But watching the view came in a distant second to keeping an eye on Carly. She sat across from him at the marble-topped table, her features tense and pale. She'd looked that way since she'd spotted the photograph of Tony. The recognition on her face at that moment had been mixed with pain, and Dan had been torn between the need to keep silent and the urge to pull her into his arms.

Emotions bubbled inside his chest: protectiveness toward Carly, fierce anger at Tony, and—God help him—jealousy toward the man who could evoke such deep emotion in her.

She was still affected by Tony, as her reaction to the photograph clearly showed. If Tony had hurt her that deeply, then she must have cared with an equal depth. He didn't know what was worse—suspecting she was a shallow, greedy hustler or knowing she'd actually been in love with his sister's husband. He realized he was angry at Carly, too, and stood up so suddenly that Arthur looked at him in surprise.

"Please excuse me. I need a breath of fresh air," Dan explained, resisting the urge to loosen his tie further and unbutton his shirt collar.

"Why certainly, my boy. Why don't we all go out on the deck for coffee?" Dan followed Arthur, ruefully thinking this would be no escape at all if everyone trooped outside with him. At least he wouldn't have to worry about Carly getting a closer look at that large seascape above the living room sofa.

They went out through the dining room's sliding glass door onto the multilevel deck, which was made of concrete and stucco like the rest of the house's exterior. Dan walked across to the railing that guarded against the sheer drop to the sea below. While the others chatted and waited for their coffee, he rested his forearms along the railing and looked down, taking in deep lungfuls of damp air. The curling white edges of the waves looked almost phosphorescent below him. Above, the indigo sky was studded with stars, like a woman's velvet-and-rhinestone evening gown.

Instead of stargazing, he should be trying to find out more about Arthur's friendship with Tony. Of course, the challenge would be doing so without letting on that he'd recognized his former brother-in-law from the photo. And without attracting Carly's attention.

God, what a tangle. Had he been completely wrong to suspect Paolo Guzman? He turned around and leaned back against the railing to watch Arthur take the silver coffee service from Conchita. Was Arthur really a retired professor, who somehow had more money than any pension could possibly provide, or was he Tony's contact? Or—he looked toward the women—was Carly still the key to Tony's whereabouts?

After tomorrow's meeting with the FBI, he would know. He'd talk to Smithy about Arthur Wright, and it wouldn't be long before they had a rundown on him. And he would try one more time to convince Smithy that they had more to gain by cooperating with Carly than by continuing to view her as a suspect. If Smithy would only see the light, he and Carly could talk at last. No more secrets—even if he was afraid of the truth.

He thanked Edith for the cup of coffee she handed him, absently refusing cream or sugar. He continued to stay at the edge of the group, letting the conversation go on around him while thoughts of tomorrow's meeting with Smithy preoccupied his mind. He didn't have a ready defense, therefore, when Edith spoke.

"The other night, I believe I heard Dan say he knew how to play bridge. Isn't that right?"

"Yes," he admitted reluctantly.

"Good, then that's settled. It's still early yet. We can finish a hand or two."

Arthur groaned. "Not that silly woman's game." He filed a string of complaints while Edith bustled back and forth, retrieving cards and lighting candles "for atmosphere."

Before sitting down at the circular wrought-iron table, Arthur drew Dan aside. "We might as well do what we can to make this game a bit more exciting, eh?" He palmed a fifty dollar bill, hiding it from Edith's view. Dan hesitated, not sure how to respond to Arthur's challenge. Luckily, Edith had spotted Arthur's gesture.

"Oh, Arthur. Can't we just enjoy a game for a change?" Arthur reluctantly put the money back in his wallet while Edith pulled out a chair and stage-managed the seating arrangements. "Carly, you partner Dan." Edith's smile was coy.

When Dan looked toward his partner, his breath caught. Her expression was lost and vulnerable, and he understood the effort she must have expended in order to appear sociable. "Are you feeling all right?" he asked quietly.

When she looked up at him, her blue eyes held an unconscious plea. He turned to Arthur and Edith. "We need a little strategy session before we start. Would you excuse us for a minute?"

Without waiting for their permission, he stood and pulled back Carly's chair, leading the way to the railing. The waves crashed against the sides of the cliffs below them, the steady sound concealing their conversation from the Wrights.

"What's the matter?" he asked.

"I'm a little tired. Too much sun yesterday, I guess," she told him. Dan didn't point out that Carly was used to the sun, accustomed as she was to swimming and sunbathing nearly every morning. Since they'd spent most of the previous afternoon in the shade, her excuse had as many holes as the smoked Swiss cheese on the tray Edith had offered with dessert.

"Why don't we leave?" he suggested gently.

"It's so early." But her protest was weak, even when she added, "Arthur and Edith will be disappointed."

"Not if we let them put their own interpretation on why we're leaving so early," he pointed out, covering Carly's hand with his own and making a show of lifting it up to his mouth for an affectionate kiss. "Edith would be especially forgiving, I suspect."

Clearly tired, she barely managed a crooked smile. They walked back across the deck, holding hands.

"I'm sorry, but we have to cancel the rest of the evening. I hope you understand." Dan let his fingers trail over Carly's wrist. Edith's eyes followed the movement avidly.

"Why, of course we understand. We do hope you'll come back soon...." Her chatter followed them all the way to the front door where they at last made their escape into the night.

* * *

Carly leaned her head back against the passenger seat of Dan's sedan and closed her eyes. She'd told him she was going to sleep on the way home, which couldn't be further from the truth. She wondered if she'd ever be able to close her eyes again. But sleeping was a ready excuse to avoid conversation and that sharp gleam in Dan's gaze. He saw too much of her, and right now, she felt too battered and bruised to put up any more defenses against his acute perception.

At least she hadn't lied about not feeling well. Thoughts banged and bumped around in her mind like the silver ball in a pinball machine, and her head ached with the effort of appearing sociable all evening. It was like being split in two, with one part of her on public display, and the other crawled tightly inside a shell of shock and fear. She felt almost betrayed by the discovery that the Wrights knew Tony. Now she felt too afraid to reach out to anyone again.

Even Dan. As the thought formed, her entire being protested that she needed him, his strength, his support. Her mind battled back and forth with the argument until she felt the car shudder to a stop. She opened her eyes, no closer to finding an answer than before.

"Feeling better?" His expression was unreadable in the dim light of the car, but the concern in his voice warmed her.

"Yes," she told him. How could she explain how she really felt? Torn between trust and wariness, overwhelmed with indecision. "Would you like to come inside?" she asked hesitantly, then admitted, "I think I need someone tonight."

He drew her into his arms and her head fit perfectly into the space between his head and shoulder. "Me, too," he said, his voice vibrating against her cheek. "That's exactly why we shouldn't."

She pulled away to look up at him, feeling tears threatening behind her eyelids at this latest rejection. She was so tired and lonely, and he was being such a damned gentleman. "I don't understand." Her words sounded a bit petulant, even to her own ears.

He laughed wryly and reached out and cupped her chin with his hand. "I'm not sure I do myself. I just think we should wait until need changes to something a little more." He tipped her chin and took her lips in an achingly sweet kiss. "We'll talk tomorrow," he said.

"Good night." Her voice was barely a whisper as she watched him walk toward his own lonely cottage for the second night in a row.

Sleep was impossible. Every time he closed his eyes, Dan saw Carly's face, vulnerable and sad, or heard Smithy's voice warning him, "Stay close to her."

He tossed and turned on his lumpy, narrow bed for hours before getting up and walking through the still-dark cottage to the cramped shower. After dressing in khaki slacks and a white cotton shirt slightly wrinkled from handwashing and line-drying, he moved his chair to the window and watched the sky change from inky black to indigo. He checked the time on the gold wristwatch he hardly bothered to wear anymore. He had to catch the morning ferry from Baja California to the mainland, where he was scheduled to meet Smithy. But first he had to find a way off Isla Linda, something that made him feel strangely reluctant.

The local ferry wouldn't be running for a couple of hours yet, but he figured he could always talk one of the fishing boat owners into taking him across for a few pesos. He took one last look around the cottage before leaving, trying to shake the crazy feeling that it might be for the last time.

Much to his surprise, the marina was already deserted, save for an ancient Indian man with blackened teeth, who apparently didn't believe in fishing before dawn. Dan suffered through a twenty-minute trip on a small boat that smelled of fish, sitting on the stained deck with his back resting against an old wooden barrel. He paid the old man and thanked him, reaching the ferry just in time.

As he stood on the deck of the ferry and watched the coastline disappear, he tried to decide how he felt. When he was a cop working on a sting operation, he used to look forward to coming out of cover. It had felt good to talk to someone, to touch base with reality and be himself again. He didn't feel that way today. All he wanted to do was return to the idyllic life he'd created on Isla Linda. To be able to watch the sun rise and set, to listen to the steady surf, to swim and laugh with Carly. That life was becoming more real to him than the one he'd left behind months ago.

His life on Isla Linda might be false, but his feelings for Carly weren't. And that was the scary part. He was ready to tell Smithy to lump this job, to leave Carly alone unless they could trace Tony through Arthur Wright. He wasn't a cop or an FBI agent, and he had no duty to complete this quest he'd undertaken.

Except his duty to his sister.

"Damn it!" He slammed his fist against the railing. It was the same old tangle he couldn't seem to work his way out of. No matter what he did—follow Smithy's orders, cut himself loose from the FBI and go undercover with Carly, or abandon his search for Tony altogether—he would feel as though he was letting someone down: Carly, Jane, his friends at the Bureau.

And then there was a little wrinkle he rarely allowed to creep into his consciousness. He was ninety-nine percent sure that Carly hadn't planned to take the money, that she'd let love blind her to Tony's purposes, and that Tony had double-crossed her at the last moment. But what if he was wrong? What if she was in on it from the start, as Smithy believed? How would that look—an ex-cop ready to stick up for an unsuccessful con?

The photograph of Tony with Arthur Wright was the only way out. If Arthur knew Tony, then maybe they could bypass Carly completely. In another hour or so, he'd be doing his best to convince Smithy.

The coastline disappeared, and he turned away from the railing to see a young couple standing a few feet away, obviously in love. *Love.* When did he start to trust that word? His parents had loved each other—and showed it by battles that nearly destroyed everything in their path, from china plates to their own children. His sister had loved her husband, and Tony betrayed her with another woman. And now he—loyal brother, straight-as-an-arrow ex-cop—fancied himself in love with that woman?

Impossible. He was concerned about her, attracted to her. Hell, why not just admit it? He wanted to get her into bed and make her forget Tony Williamson ever existed.

He left the ferry in an even worse mood than he'd boarded with, finding a bus that was overcrowded and hot to take him to Hermosillo. He spotted Smithy seated at a table near the rear of the café the FBI agent had chosen for the meeting.

If it weren't for the fact that most of the faces surrounding him were Hispanic or Indian, Jedidiah Smith would have been unnoticeable. Smithy had gotten his nickname because he looked more like a proper English butler than a man of action. Balding, bespectacled, and nondescript, wearing a plain dark suit even on this hot day, Smithy nodded to Dan.

Dan started across the room. No one would even guess that Smithy had the highest ranking in his class at West Point, that he'd served two tours in 'Nam, or that he held a black belt in Tae Kwon Do. He blended into the crowd like a chameleon, an ability that was a true asset for working undercover. Dan had met him when they'd cooperated on a counterfeiting case in L.A.

Their greetings were brief. After this strategy session, Smithy had to return to Phoenix by evening. Without preamble, Smithy shook Dan's hand and said, "What have you got for me?"

Carly overslept, missing her usual morning swim after tossing and turning all night. She'd had dreams of Dan on the beach that mingled with nightmares about Tony. Seeing the photograph of the man who'd betrayed her brought back her old feelings of humiliation and shame. When the first rays of sunlight peeped in, she'd buried herself underneath the covers, wishing she could hide forever. But there was no safe hiding place, as she'd begun to realize ever since she'd received the letter from her new attorney.

She finally opened her eyes, unable to ignore the growing heat and bright sunshine any longer. The half-forgotten nightmares still pulled at her as she dressed in her swimsuit. Today she needed the cool water to clear her head. She headed for the beach, then changed her mind and walked up the path to Dan's cabin instead, to ask if he wanted to join her. Assuming he wasn't already off somewhere painting, although it seemed as though he rarely opened a tube of paint anymore.

She looked over her shoulder as she waited for the door to open, her gaze scanning the beach. It was deserted, and there was no answer to her repeated knocking. Tentatively, she pushed open the door and stepped inside. She saw a square of notepaper—the same kind she'd used to pen her thank-you to Dan—on the small table near the kitchen, as though he'd guessed she would enter the cabin to look for him. Too curious to be embarrassed, she read the note. All it said was that he'd gone to the other side of the island to paint. She walked to the window, wondering how he'd managed to get that far without his car. Then she realized his easel was still here, too.

Her forehead wrinkled in puzzlement. The first painting Dan had completed was leaning against the opposite wall, so the one covered on the easel must be new. Chuckling over her embarrassment the last time she'd been caught snooping, she pulled back the paint-stained sheet to reveal another seascape, this one in moonlight. It reminded her of the nights they'd spent near the water, beginning with the first night Dan had walked her home. Then she'd stared out at the ocean, wondering if she would ever have a normal life with a man like him. Now she was almost certain her dreams had a chance to come true. She'd know for sure after today, because she was determined to tell him exactly how she'd ended up on Isla Linda. She couldn't carry the secret any longer because it was the only thing keeping them apart.

Her gaze traveled over the painting, trying to place the scene. The way the moonlight made a path on the water made her think of the night they swam and played on the beach. Memories followed one after the other, as she thought of all the times they'd spent together. A picture of the afternoon she and Dan had spent at Hummingbird Cove popped into her mind, and she remembered that it had been part of her dreams this morning.

In the dream, Dan had been speaking perfect Spanish to the little boy, Mateo. She frowned as she realized that part hadn't been a dream. He'd called Mateo his little man—*in Spanish.*

Her breath stopped. It wasn't the sort of phrase a tourist would pick up in a few days on the island. Either Dan was an amazingly fast learner, or he'd lied to her about knowing the language.

But why would Dan lie?

Had he told her that he couldn't speak Spanish just so she'd have to spend more time with him? Or were his reasons even more underhanded?

She swallowed back the pressing feeling that was rising in her throat and tried to calm herself. The shock of seeing that photograph of Tony Williamson last night was making her doubt everyone.

She tried to stop giving rise to all these suspicious thoughts, but her mind refused to cooperate, digging up one questionable phrase or gesture after the other. For example, she thought of the night before when Dan had ushered her quickly out of the Wrights' living room. They'd been standing underneath a painting remarkably similar to this one.

She stared at Dan's signature in the right-hand corner of the canvas. Slowly, her hand reached out to touch the painting, lightly tracing the bumps and ridges of waves and rocks made by the heavy application of oils. Her mother used to paint as a hobby, and Carly remembered that oils took several days to dry. She trailed her fingers toward Dan's bold signature in the corner, snatching her hand away at the shocking dampness.

She stared at the smeared paint on her fingers, then at the blurred signature. It was possible that Dan had completed the painting days ago and waited for it to dry before signing it.

But she knew with a sinking heart that he had never painted this picture. He'd bought it from the same artist who'd painted the scene in Arthur and Edith's living room, then painted over the signature and added his own. Why?

The answer seemed quite obvious. Dan Turner wasn't an artist at all. Someone had sent him to watch her. But who? The FBI, her stepfather, or Tony?

And which one was most dangerous?

Chapter Eight

Carly ran from Dan's cottage as though pursued by a demon. But this demon was inside her. She was suffering from that old, familiar plague—her inability to discern between lies and the truth. While she might not be able to hide from herself, she could hide from Dan. She had to get away.

It was nearly noon when she threw open the door of her cottage and dashed across the room, pulling her tapestry-patterned luggage out from underneath the bed. She tossed handfuls of clothing into the suitcase, unable to keep from thinking how carefully she'd packed the same case nearly a year ago for her weekend with Tony.

And now another man had turned out to be false.

She drove the destructive thoughts from her mind. She didn't have time for self-recriminations if she wanted to get out of here before Dan returned from wherever he'd gone. She sank to her knees to pick up a pair of shorts that had fallen onto the floor, but she couldn't seem to pull herself up afterward.

So she knelt there and allowed the tears to fall silently down her cheeks. When she realized she was wasting time, she stood and found a sundress to pull over her white swimsuit. If she hurried, she could catch the next ferry to Baja California. But first she needed to stop at Paolo's to tell him she wouldn't be coming to work.

She finished filling her suitcase with as much as she could cram into it, then splashed cool water over her tear-streaked cheeks. As she walked along the beach, half dragging the heavy luggage, the palm trees looked familiar and dear, no longer the prison bars they'd once seemed. She felt tears threatening again and strived for a calm expression before arriving at the Guzmans'.

It proved more difficult than she'd expected. One look at her eyes and Paolo demanded, *"¿Qué pasa?* What's wrong, Carlita?"

Lupe's plump hands clutched at her ever-present rosary, betraying her worry, and Carly gave up on the story she'd concocted about needing to go to the mainland on business. Instead, she said simply, "I have to leave the island as soon as possible. I don't have time to explain everything."

"You will come back, *sí?"* Lupe asked.

"I don't know if I can come back here or not," she told them honestly. "I hope so."

Paolo's eyes were sharp, and she knew he was thinking of the things they'd never discussed in detail—the letters that came for her from the States, the newspaper article about the embezzlement, her lack of a visa or work permit. Paolo must have guessed what would happen to her if she returned to the U.S. "Do you need anything?" he asked her.

"No, I'll be fine."

"Stay for *la comida* with us, at least," Lupe said.

"No, I don't have time to eat. I can't take a chance on missing the ferry. There won't be another one for several hours. I have to leave now."

Lupe shot a pleading look toward Paolo, who said, "I will take you myself. Come, Carly."

He picked up her suitcase and headed for the marina, where he still kept the small fishing boat his father had used. Carly followed, stopping for a moment when Lupe ran up behind her to press a bag of fresh tortillas into her hand and give her a hug.

It wasn't until they were halfway across the narrow channel of water that Paolo asked, "Where are you going, Carlita?"

"It's better that you don't know," she told him, "in case someone tries to question you." She thought of Dan and felt a surge of anger. *Good—at least she was through with the tears.* "Besides," she added gently, "I'm not sure where I'll end up."

As they sped toward the rocky coast of Baja California, Carly turned for a last glimpse of Isla Linda. The island looked like a child's plaything from here, a disk of sand and fuzzy green trees, like something from a model train set. She said a silent goodbye, then turned and looked ahead.

"What do you mean, you don't know where she is?" Dan faced Paolo Guzman across the bar, which the older man polished slowly with an old dishrag.

"She left around noon. She didn't say where she was going." He stared at Dan coldly. "Perhaps you know why?"

Dan backed away. Paolo's animosity was almost palpable. "No," he said hoarsely, although he had a pretty good idea. Carly must have guessed he was meeting with the FBI. And she'd ran. He turned and walked out of the cantina, the implications of her flight running through his mind. Only a few hours ago, he'd managed to talk Smithy into entertaining the possibility that Carly might be innocent. Now he wasn't so sure that she was innocent himself.

How did she find out about his trip to the mainland? Could Tony have found a way to tip her off? He always seemed to be one step ahead of the FBI. Was Carly running to him even now? Dan wondered if he should have pressed Paolo harder. It seemed pretty obvious that Paolo was involved, too.

"Damn it." He stopped, knowing he should turn and go back to the cantina to call Smithy and tell him of Carly's escape. On the other hand, if Tony knew what the FBI was up to, talking to them would only tip Tony off. And then there was the possibility that Dan had stumbled onto a whole island of liars, people who might want to protect their little hideaway at any cost.

He looked around him, seeing the sleepy little cluster of houses and businesses and finding it hard to believe something so sinister. Still, he couldn't afford to trust anyone. Including Carly, assuming he would find her.

He headed resolutely toward the cottages. Smithy would just have to wait. If he called now, there was no telling what the FBI agent might do to keep Carly from disappearing again. Dan was going to find her himself if he had to turn over every rock in Mexico. She had a few hours head start on him, but she couldn't go far before he caught up. She was much too recognizable—a beautiful young Anglo woman traveling alone was bound to attract attention.

So, after checking Carly's cabin for any clue that might tell him where she'd gone, he left Isla Linda for the second time that day, in another fishing boat bound for Baja California. He had to stop her before she got to Tony. He knew this was personal, but then it had been that way ever since he'd decided to find Tony for his sister Janie. He'd turned in his badge just so he could be the one to bring in his erstwhile brother-in-law, like an old-time bounty hunter. He had every intention of getting his man.

And his woman, too.

Carly stared numbly out the sliding glass door at the narrow strip of beach visible from her third-story window. The

hotel was one of the cheapest she could find in Cabo San
Lucas, the beautiful resort town at the tip of Baja California. In her purse she had a ticket to the mainland, which
took almost all the money she had saved after months of
working at the cantina. She had wanted to get as far from
Baja California and Dan as she possibly could. She had
enough pesos left for breakfast, and then she'd have to think
of a way to earn more without a work permit or visa.

She turned back to the tidy but small room. The decor
was uninspired. A still-life print hung above the full-size
bed, and a small table did double duty as a nightstand. A
single chair stood next to the table. At least the room was
scrupulously clean, which was more than she could say for
some of the less expensive hotels she had looked at.

The soonest available flight for the mainland left at nine
in the morning, but that was fine with Carly, because she
couldn't have gone another mile tonight. She'd spent the day
in boats, trains, and buses, traveling third-class most of the
way, without air-conditioning. Between La Paz and Todos
Santos, she'd had to share her seat with a chicken—a prize-
winner, according to the young man who owned her. He had
stood in the aisle so that the chicken could ride in comfort.

Right now Carly was hot, tired, and hungry enough to
wish she'd thought of smuggling the chicken away with her.
She collapsed onto the too-soft bed and counted her money
again, wondering if it would be enough for a light supper.
Not if she wanted to eat in the morning, she decided. She
thought ruefully of the millions of dollars sitting around in
her trust fund, doing nothing but collecting interest and
dust.

In a few months she would be twenty-five, an heiress,
unless Robert Daimler could prove, according to the pro-
visions in her mother's will, that she was unfit to inherit. In
that case, of course, the money would be his. Right now—
as she sat in a hotel, on the run, counting her last pesos—
that outcome sounded like a certainty. It was more than

possible that Robert Daimler had sent Dan to make sure she wouldn't try to collect.

She sat up and stared out the glass at the growing twilight. Possible, but not likely. Daimler was a thug. A rich, well-groomed, charming thug with connections to the underworld. Dan wasn't the type of man to do business with her stepfather. No matter what lies he'd told her, he couldn't have pretended his sympathetic reaction when she'd told him of her stepfather's advances.

Stop it, she told herself. Why was she still trying to make excuses for Dan? Somewhere she'd gained a falsely idealistic picture of Dan Turner that refused to go away. He'd lied to her, even pretended to love her.

Love? Yes—he may never have used the word, but then neither had she.

Even after everything that had happened, there was no question in her mind. Dan Turner was a man of honor—she knew that. He didn't work for her stepfather and probably not for Tony, either. There was no way Tony could have known that she was thinking about returning to the U.S. to testify. He probably figured her chances of implicating him were slim; he was very likely lying in a comfortable beach chair somewhere, with an orange and vodka in his hand and a string of native beauties waiting on him as though he were a sheikh. Carly hoped grimly that there was sand in his screwdriver.

But if Dan wasn't working for Robert or Tony, who did that leave besides the FBI? Dan had to be some kind of cop. It still didn't excuse his lies, not when he knew how she felt about him. It must have been obvious to him that she'd fallen for him. She groaned and fell back onto the bed, thinking of all the times she'd practically gift-wrapped herself, and he'd still rejected her.

Perhaps it was part of his game to get her to fall in love with him. If so, his plan had worked. Her instincts had really failed her this time. Dan Turner was her biggest, most glorious mistake of all.

Dan knocked on the door and waited, hoping the money he'd flashed at the front-desk clerk was enough. He'd left cash all over Baja California, from rail porters to bus drivers to that supercilious desk clerk downstairs. He was down to his last few dollars, so this was the end of the trail, for now at least.

He knocked again, then looked up and down the hall before slipping his credit card into the space between the door and the frame. Fortunately, Carly had chosen a third-rate hotel with precious little security. He worked the card carefully, trying not to damage it. He'd probably need to use it later to get more cash.

Opening the door was shamefully easy. The small room was simply furnished, and a suitcase lay open on the bed. The muted tapestry fabric looked like the suitcase he'd seen stored beneath Carly's bed, but he couldn't be certain. He closed the door behind him, but before he could check to see if any of the clothing tumbling out of the case was hers, he heard a shocked gasp. He turned to see her standing by the bathroom doorway in nothing but a towel.

Her hair was wet, and water beaded across her shoulders. A half-dozen responses clicked through his mind at the sight of her—anger that she'd led him on such a merry chase, relief that he'd found her, guilt that he had to take her back. Crowding out all the other responses was the desire to pull the towel from her and take her into his arms.

He was incapable of speech for several moments. When he finally found his voice again, the words came out far harsher than he'd intended. "Are you alone?"

"Not anymore," she said crossly. "If you wouldn't mind stepping outside for a few minutes, I'd like to get dressed."

He allowed his gaze to stray just a few centimeters from her eyes, enough so that his peripheral vision could feast on the soft glow of her shoulders. "And give you the opportunity to run again? Not a chance, sweetheart."

She turned away at his sarcastic endearment, and he felt a moment of regret. He knew she would hardly try to escape by climbing out on the balcony and jumping down three stories, but now that he'd found her, he didn't want to leave her. He felt a flash of anger at his own weakness.

"Is Tony meeting you here?" he asked harshly.

She looked at him stonily, her chin high, as she pulled the towel tighter. She succeeded only in drawing Dan's gaze to the swell of her breasts above the white terry cloth.

"Here." He reached into the suitcase and pulled out a handful of crumpled clothing. "Put something on." *Before I rip that towel off,* he thought. He tossed the clothes at her, and they fell to the floor in a soft heap. He could tell by the way she clenched the towel tightly with both hands that she wasn't about to let go to pick them up.

She continued to stare at him silently, making him feel like an unreasonable fool.

"You can use the bathroom," he said. "I'll turn around." He heard her open and close the door, leaving him with his tortured thoughts. He glanced around the room. There was no sign of Tony, although he hadn't expected there to be. He'd also shown a picture of him to the desk clerk, who had declared in simpering Spanish that she'd never seen such a handsome man. He hadn't appreciated being reminded of how handsome Tony was, or how easily the man could charm any female that crossed his path.

The way he'd managed to charm Carly....

He paced the floor. Carly was taking so long in the bathroom that he wanted to reach in and drag her out. Trying to convince himself he had an entirely different kind of hunger, he reached for a flyer by the phone. This hotel might not be first-class, but at least it had room service, limited as the short list was. He ordered quickly, reading off the first several items on the menu without thinking. Then he went back to waiting. At last he saw the crack of light below the bathroom door go out.

As soon as she opened the door, wearing a short lavender silk robe, he could see that she'd been crying. He felt a stab of guilt again, then strengthened his resolve by picturing his sister Janie. She'd cried a lot, too, he reminded himself.

"Are you meeting Tony Williamson here?" he asked again.

"No. I haven't seen him for almost a year," she answered mechanically, walking over to sit on the edge of the bed.

Dan stayed where he was, believing height was his only advantage. Even after he'd seen the torn letter, even after she had run away, he realized that he still harbored the hope that she might be innocent. "Why did you leave Isla Linda?" he asked, impatient with himself and with his weakness more than he was with her.

Before she could answer, he pressed her with more questions. "Did you do it? Did you plot with Tony to take the money?"

"No." She sat with her hands in her lap, looking up at him stonily, and it was all he could do to hang tough.

"According to the MIS department's computer records, that transaction was made from your workstation using your password."

"Tony used it while I was on the phone. He said he needed to make a quick transfer, and I gave him my access code so he wouldn't have to go all the way back to his own office on the other side of the building."

So simple, so pat. Either Tony was the laziest and luckiest damn con in the world, or Carly was the most accomplished liar.

"You left the office early that day. Together. The receptionist remembers seeing you." He phrased it as a question, crossing his arms over his chest and leaning back against the wall so she wouldn't know how important her answer was to him.

"Yes." She didn't elaborate, and he cursed inwardly. She was forcing him to drag every piece of information out of her. But his next question reflected none of his impatience. "Why did you leave with Tony?"

She looked down at her lap, where her hands toyed with the edge of her silk robe. "We were going on a weekend cruise in Mazatlán."

"But you ended up instead on Isla Linda. Apparently that cruise wasn't what it seemed."

"A lot of things weren't as they seemed. Including Tony. I'm a slow learner, you see. It's taken me some time to realize that men can't be trusted."

Women, either, he wanted to shout back, catching himself just in time. God, what had happened to his professional detachment? Was this how it had been for his parents, this wanting to stab each other with words, then wishing you could make it all up with kisses?

"I was going to go back to the States soon and tell my attorney all of this."

He looked at her skeptically. "Then why did you run?"

She shrugged. "For one thing, I thought Daimler might have sent you to keep me here so he could get my trust fund." She explained the clause in her will, something Dan already knew. "Then I realized you weren't Daimler's type."

"And for another?"

"For another, I thought..." She looked out the window even though there was nothing to see. With the light next to the bed turned on, the expanse of glass reflected the small hotel room like a mirror. Dan could watch Carly's face as she finished. "I thought I was in love with you."

He had to strain to catch the quietly spoken words, but he knew she was telling the truth. Her revelation caught him by surprise, taking away all his breath to ask any more questions. Leave it to Smithy and the FBI, he thought. He was

afraid to ask the most important question, the one that the
FBI probably wouldn't ask: How far had her relationship
with Tony gone? He knew it hardly mattered to Janie anymore. She'd gotten her divorce, and was managing without
child support. But it mattered to him.

She continued to stare out the window, and his gaze traveled over the silk robe, noting how it clung to her soft
curves. *Jesus. He had to get a grip on himself.* A loud knock
startled him until he remembered ordering room service. He
tipped the uniformed waiter and asked him to bill the meal
to the room. He still had some money in his savings account, but he intended to bill every last cent of this to the
Bureau.

"I got plenty for two," he told Carly. "I hope you like
potluck. I can't remember what I ordered, except that I ordered a lot."

"I'm not hungry."

He knew she was lying by the way her gaze followed his
movements as he lifted one of the covered dishes and began
to eat. "Mmm. Pork chops. My favorite. Sure you don't
want any?"

She shook her head. "Am I under arrest?"

"No." He saw her shoulders sag with relief. "But I can't
let you go, either." She looked up at him, puzzled. "I'm
staying here with you tonight."

Her puzzlement changed to shock, and he cut off her
protest. "Help yourself to the food," he told her, finishing
off a pork chop before rising to his feet. "I have to step
outside for a minute. Don't try anything."

He couldn't put off calling Smithy any longer. It was his
case, after all, and now that Dan had found Carly, he'd do
anything he could to try to get Smithy's assurances that she
would be safe.

"Like what? Jump out the window?" she asked, her
frustration showing.

At least she wasn't sad anymore. He'd hated that teary look because it made him feel like a jerk. He knew she wouldn't eat with him there, so he waited until her gaze went to the food again before he walked to the door.

"It'll be all right," he told her, wishing it were that simple. "You'll be fine," he added with more assurance. Carly would be fine, he thought as he shut the door behind him. He wasn't so sure about himself.

The impulse to run warred with hunger. Carly watched the door, knowing Dan was probably nearby. Even if she could escape him, there was no point. Now that she'd told her side of the story to him, it was easier to go back to the States than to keep on running.

She hadn't expected him to be so cool, though. He barely reacted at all to her confession. The only time he'd shown any hint of sympathy was in ordering all this food and leaving so she could eat in privacy. She went over to the small table, still crowded with dishes, and started pulling off the silver-domed lids. There was enough food here to feed an army: an entire chicken, fries, salad greens, a hamburger. She thought about not eating any of it, but hunger clenched at her stomach like a fist. This was no time to be proud.

She shoveled food into her mouth, barely tasting it, as though it might be days before she'd be able to eat again. She tried to picture the next few days as best she could. Would they handcuff her and read her rights when she crossed the border? Would reporters and photographers be waiting with microphones and cameras?

She could face the publicity, even the ordeal of a trial. The hardest thing was to face Dan's lack of concern. She hadn't run from the law as much as she'd run from the knowledge he was only using her. She'd grown so used to that tender caring. And now she'd have to travel with him, share this room even, as though he were a stranger. Nothing could be harder than that.

Except prison—her mind went blank. It wouldn't really come to that, would it? She remembered what the attorney had written: *Trust in the law and hope Tony will be found.*

Was Dan looking for Tony? Her fork stilled as she remembered the photo of Tony with Arthur Wright. Had Dan noticed that photo? Could he trace Tony through the Wrights? As the questions crowded her mind, she began to see Dan as a potential ally. Would he help her find the man who had framed her? She felt a rising sense of excitement at the prospect. Somehow she had to convince him that she was innocent, that Tony was the one he needed to find before he took her back to the States.

But when Dan reentered, her hopes faltered at his shuttered expression. She tried to warm him up with a quick smile. "Thank you for ordering enough for me. I was hungry," she admitted. "I'll pay you back, of course."

"No problem. The meal is courtesy of the U.S. Government."

She felt a flash of resentment at his offhandedness. He was making jokes when her entire life was about to change. Didn't he have any idea what she was going through? "Can't they spring for another room while they're at it?" she asked.

"I tried to find a bigger room or another hotel. They're all booked up. Some kind of convention," he said.

Her gaze flew to the bed.

"Don't worry. I'll sleep in the chair," he told her as he sat down on the edge of the bed across from her. She was still sitting in the chair, inches away from the table. He raised one eyebrow at the remnants of food. Carly followed his gaze and flushed.

"At least we've got room service," he said with a brief grin.

They fell silent for a moment before Carly spoke again. "What happens next?" she asked, trying not to show how scared she was.

"Next, we get some sleep."

"You don't have to sleep in this chair. I'm sure I'd be perfectly safe sleeping with you. It's fairly obvious you don't want to touch me," she said.

Heat flashed in his eyes. "Oh, I'd like to touch you all right." He reached out and pulled her onto the bed beside him. "Want to know where?"

He bent and murmured into her ear, hot, forbidden words that shocked her. His voice was low and husky, and she felt it echo inside her. Just when she knew she couldn't stand to listen another moment without pulling him closer, he put her away from him.

His expression was calm enough, but as she stared, she could see the unsteady rise and fall of his chest and the pulse beating at the side of his throat. He wasn't as unaffected as he pretended. While part of her was gratified that his physical response to her was real, another part was hurt by his rough passion. The tenderness he'd shown before was gone, and he was acting almost as though he hated her, she realized.

Then she understood. *He didn't believe her.*

She met his steady gaze and said, "This doesn't have anything to do with the law, does it? Keeping me here, treating me this way? It's because you don't believe me."

"Believe what? That you were naive enough to fall for Tony's lies?" He shrugged.

"I fell for yours," she pointed out.

He had the decency to look ashamed, a sign that gave Carly hope she might be able to reach him. He released her arm, stood and strode to the chair, slapping the sagging cushion into shape before turning to look at her again. His voice was rough. "If you don't get into that bed now, I'll toss you in myself."

She crawled under the covers and cast him a challenging glare, hoping he would suffer the torment of the damned in that small chair. But when she was still lying awake, staring at the ceiling, he was snoring softly. She pounded the pillow, an echo of his earlier action, and tried to still the nervous beating of her heart.

This scenario was so far from what she'd imagined. She'd thought that Dan would support her—that he would stand beside her when she decided to throw herself on the mercy of the law. Instead, he was beside her to turn her in, probably getting himself a fat raise and a promotion in the process.

She hadn't even asked him about the FBI, she realized. Wasn't she supposed to check his badge or something? Had the extradition order gone through without her knowledge? She felt tears threatening, but she resolutely held them at bay. Her fate was in her own hands, after all. Feeling stronger, she finally fell into a deep sleep.

A knock at the door woke her up not long after the morning sunlight began to penetrate the heavy curtains Dan had pulled shut sometime during the night. She threw back the covers, glanced down at the lacy nightgown she had purchased for her weekend with Tony, and quickly pulled the covers back up. She looked around for Dan and saw the empty chair before noticing the sound of the shower running. She pulled a sheet around her and went to answer the door, her stomach already anticipating the breakfast Dan must have ordered from room service.

But instead of the uniformed waiter she expected, a slight, balding man dressed in a somber suit stood on the other side. His gaze took in her bare shoulders and feet, then went past her into the room, resting finally on the tousled bed.

"Carly Dawson?" he asked, looking at her only briefly before stepping past her into the room.

She was too startled to even protest. "Yes, I'm Carly Dawson."

"I'm Agent Smith. With the FBI," he added at her startled look.

She stood and stared at him stupidly for a moment. "If you're with the FBI, then who's—"

"Thank God, I'd forgotten what a real shower felt like."

Both of them turned to see Dan emerge from the bathroom, dressed in jeans and rubbing his hair vigorously with a towel. When he pulled the towel away and spotted Agent Smith, he went still.

"Smithy," he greeted. "Thanks for coming."

Carly felt a growing sense of unreality. She turned to Dan and said, "I thought you were with the FBI."

"Nope."

She stared at him, feeling duped and wondering if he'd had any jurisdiction over her at all. "Then who are you?"

"I used to be a cop with the L.A.P.D. But that's not why I'm here. I'm Tony Williamson's brother-in-law. He was married to my sister, Janie."

It took Carly a while to process the information. When she finally put together that Dan's beloved sister was married to the man Carly had traveled to Mexico with, she understood at last what was behind that cold look in Dan's light green eyes.

He thought she'd slept with his sister's husband.

Chapter Nine

"As long as you two have already met, I'll just go and get dressed," Dan said, anxious to get away from the expression of horrified realization on Carly's face.

Back in the bathroom, he rubbed at the steam clouding the mirror. He no longer had any illusions left. Or maybe he should call them *delusions*. The look on Carly's face had told him all he needed to know: she had come to Mexico to spend the weekend with his sister's husband. He'd known it intellectually for quite some time now, but some part of him—some stupidly naive part of him—had persisted in thinking of her as a completely innocent victim. He'd wanted to believe in her just as he'd wanted to believe in love.

He braced his hands against the cultured marble sink and repeated the word that was so hard to say, even with no one to hear it but himself: *Love*.

He'd grown up mistrusting the word, seeing how his parents "loved" each other. He'd never said it to a woman, even though there had been two or three times in his life when a woman had grown tired of waiting for him to say it and had left. *Love.* His lips silently formed the word as he stared into the mirror. He looked at his reflection, seeing the truth of it in his own face.

He was in love with Carly Dawson.

Even knowing that she'd been behind his sister's hurt, he wanted to protect her, to save her from the judgment he'd seen in Smithy's face. But how could he convince Smithy she was innocent if he wasn't sure himself?

Stop, he commanded, whisking off the towel draped over his shoulders. He hadn't even bothered to pack in his haste to catch up with Carly, so he'd dressed in the same jeans he'd worn the day before. He reached for his shirt, which he'd left hanging over the doorknob to steam out the wrinkles, but his hands hesitated on the buttons. Maybe he shouldn't have followed her at all. Maybe he should have let her slip away.

Then he pictured Carly running all over Mexico to get away from him, from Tony, from her stepfather. He rejected the images that went along with that thought. At least here she was safe, although she probably didn't realize it yet. He couldn't have left her to run. Nor could he go back to the States with her.

Not with the woman who had shattered his sister's life. He smiled ironically at his reflection. *Duty, loyalty, honor.* He may have left the force, but those words were still engraved in his psyche.

But didn't he have a duty to Carly, too? *Yes.* The word was like a cry from his soul. Yes. He would do his best to persuade Smithy that Carly deserved immunity, that she wasn't guilty of any crime except loving the wrong man. Then he would continue his search for Tony here in Mexico while Smithy went back to the States with Carly. He told himself it was the right way, the only one that made sense. The only way he could satisfy his duty to everyone: the FBI, Carly, Janie.

And to himself?

He turned his back on the question and reentered the room, none of his inner struggle showing on his face. Carly was seated on the room's sole chair—the one where he'd spent the night before. She was still wrapped in the sheet from the bed, but he'd caught a glimpse of her nightgown on his way to the shower this morning. For his sake, he was glad Smithy was here.

Smithy sat perched on the edge of the unmade bed, losing some of his dignity in his obvious distaste for the situation. Dan would have been amused if it weren't for the wide-eyed, desperate look Carly shot his way. He felt like a jerk for holing up in the bathroom and leaving her in this situation.

"Why don't you get dressed now?" he suggested gently.

She stood and brushed past him, and he had to force himself to keep from reaching out and pulling her into his arms. When the bathroom door shut with a click, he glared at Smithy.

The agent smiled implacably. "I didn't realize you had to go quite this far to bring in the suspect." He looked at the bed, where tumbled sheets and pillows made it obvious that Carly had spent a restless night. "Should I offer you a bonus?"

Dan itched to punch Smithy's face in, wondering how he could have considered this man a friend. He glared and said, "It's not how it looks."

"Right."

But Smithy's grin faded as Dan stepped closer, murder in his eyes. "I believe we have some business to discuss. What are the FBI's plans for Carly?"

"You know we can't arrest her—yet. The extradition order is pending."

Dan felt a chill. "She's spoken with an attorney about returning," he said, deciding that was all Smithy needed to know about the letter. "She made a stupid mistake. That doesn't make her a dangerous criminal."

"She's made a lot of stupid mistakes," Smithy commented, reminding Dan of Carly's juvenile record.

"All inadmissible in court. She had a tough childhood."

"An heiress? A rich girl who lived in a multimillion-dollar home in one of the most exclusive areas in Phoenix? A spoiled brat who defied her parents at every turn? Her stepfather has already expressed his concern to our office in Phoenix."

Dan snorted. "I just bet he has. All Robert Daimler is worried about is her trust fund."

"Of course. That's his job. He's the fund's administrator. That's why we thought she might try to surface before too long, to get her hands on the money."

"If she'd taken two million, she wouldn't need the money," Dan pointed out patiently. "You know who gets the trust fund if she forfeits."

"Robert Daimler. Why?" Smithy's impatience was visible. "Look, we went over this yesterday in Hermosillo. I checked into both Daimler's and Arthur Wright's backgrounds. Everything you told me matched up. But they didn't run off to Mexico with two million dollars. She's still wanted for suspicion of embezzlement, and I've still got to do my job."

Carly could hear raised masculine voices from the adjoining room. She sat on the edge of the bathtub, wearing a short-skirted sundress. She'd taken her time getting dressed, showering and using the small bar of soap to wash her hair. The hotel didn't provide shampoo, and she hadn't brought any of her own. She thought nostalgically of the first-class hotels she used to stay in whenever she traveled, elegant places where guests were treated like royalty.

Then she thought of her cozy little cottage on Isla Linda and felt a wave of homesickness that surprised her. She realized she wasn't sure where home was anymore. It certainly wasn't the sprawling house on Camelback Mountain, where Robert Daimler still lived. Nor was it her apartment in downtown Phoenix, which had been relet months ago.

Still pondering the issue, she lingered in the bathroom, unwilling to go back to Smithy's impersonal gray-eyed gaze. Even Dan's scorn was better than that. She was able to catch only a word or two of their heated exchange. She heard her own name, then Robert Daimler's, just enough to know that Dan was defending her. A sense of gratitude, mixed with relief, swept through her.

He cared a little, at least. Oh, she knew he wanted her. No woman, even one as inexperienced as she was, could fail to see the heat that entered those green eyes whenever he looked at her. But she hadn't been sure of his caring, not since yesterday. She had to count on that—it was her salvation, not only against Smithy and the weight of the FBI, but also against her own despair. He might not like it, he might not even realize it, but he cared what happened to her.

Now all she had to do was convince him that she was guiltless.

She stood, feeling more confident, and opened the door. The men's conversation ceased.

"Can the condemned woman at least order a last meal?" she asked with forced lightness. "I'm starving."

Dan glared at Smithy, seated across from him on the bed. "It's a good plan," the agent defended.

"It's a lousy plan." Dan's gaze strayed through the sliding glass door to the balcony, where Carly sat with the remains of the enormous breakfast she'd ordered. He had listened in disbelief as she'd recited a list of menu items over the phone.

Smithy had insisted on privacy for this conversation, and yet the agent wouldn't let Carly out of his sight. She leaned back against the side of the balcony in a narrow strip of shade that was decreasing by the minute.

"Can't you take her back with you to the States, where it's safer?"

"You know I can't arrest her here in Mexico. I doubt she'd go with me willingly," he said. "She doesn't even seem to like me. You, on the other hand . . ." He looked at Dan speculatively. "Besides, where could she be any safer than with you?

Dan turned back to glare at Smithy. Even though the same thought had crossed his mind—several times—he knew how hard it would be to spend that much time with Carly and not . . .

He forced his mind back to the discussion with Smithy. "I don't work for the FBI. I can drop this anytime."

"Do you want to?"

"Yes," he practically shouted, noting by the lift of Carly's head that she must have heard him through the glass doorway. "No," he admitted, more quietly this time. "But I don't like the way this is playing out. The FBI doesn't usually work this way. This whole situation is highly irregular."

"Irregular?" Smithy echoed, clearly amused at Dan's choice of words. "We've always been prepared to improvise when the situation calls for it. I didn't know you were so squeamish. Just how badly do you want to find Tony Williamson?"

Dan's gaze strayed back to Carly, following a bead of perspiration that trailed down her throat and disappeared into the scooped neckline of her tropical print dress. He bit back a groan and looked away. He thought of Tony hurting Janie, then Carly, the two women he cared about more than any others. "Real bad," he admitted. "Tony Williamson should be locked up where he can't con anyone else."

"The FBI wants the same thing," Smithy said quickly. "You just need to get him somewhere we can arrest him. International waters, like we planned. It shouldn't be that hard, with the right bait."

Carly, Dan thought, feeling slightly sick. He nodded reluctantly.

"Then you'll put up with a little irregularity. I can't work out the details until the rest of the team gets here, but I assure you that everything will be choreographed like *Swan Lake.* We'll coach both of you. It's important that the whole thing appears absolutely genuine. I'm sure you won't mind going along with it."

"Pretending to be Carly's lover?" The words came out rough, and Dan cleared his throat.

"Tony got everything but the girl. I have a feeling his ego would like to have another chance."

"I'd like to ask Carly about it first."

"She doesn't have a choice."

"What about me?"

Smithy shrugged. "Like you said, you can quit anytime." He glanced at his watch. "I need to make a phone call. Why don't you take her for a walk?"

"Carly," Dan said shortly.

"Pardon me?"

"Her name is Carly. Miss Dawson if you like. Just quit talking about her like she's a piece of office equipment."

"Whatever you say," Smithy said, smiling thinly. "I only hope I don't need to remind you that a good cop doesn't get involved."

"I'm not a cop anymore," Dan said as he stood. He turned his back on Smithy and unlatched the sliding glass door to join Carly on the balcony. The heat hit him like a blast from a foundry furnace. "Jeez," he said. "Why didn't you tell us it was getting this uncomfortable out here?"

She shrugged. "I'm used to it. Hurricane season hasn't even started yet. Wait until the humidity picks up and—"

She stopped, and Dan knew she'd just remembered that things had changed.

"Let's go for a walk," he said abruptly.

"Where?" she asked, but her question was without curiosity. "I've never been outside Isla Linda."

"Anywhere. Just away from here."

They walked through the hotel room, and she and Smithy studiously ignored each other. The downstairs lobby was packed with people wearing nametags, and Dan guided Carly through the crowd. They walked for a while before stopping at an open-air café. Dan ordered cold drinks, and they watched the crowd of tourists and honeymooners stroll past on their way to the beach or back to a cruise ship. It seemed odd to see people going happily about their lives while his and Carly's hung in the balance.

He told her about Smithy's plan, that the two of them return to the island and try to learn about Tony Williamson through the Wrights.

"How?"

"That's where it gets sticky. Smithy is setting up some kind of plan with the other agents. Because they don't have extradition, everything will have to be coordinated carefully."

"But you and I are supposed to carry on as though nothing has happened?"

"Not exactly." Dan shifted uncomfortably in his seat. "Smithy wants us to tell anyone who asks that we spent the weekend together here in Cabo."

"He wants us to pretend to be lovers," she said bluntly. "Won't that be a stretch for you?"

Dan didn't trust himself to answer. He finished his iced tea and set the glass down on the table.

"I don't suppose you'd consider letting me go?" she asked.

He actually thought about it for a moment. It would be so easy. All he'd have to do was leave the table for a few minutes and return to find her seat empty. Panic filled him just thinking about it.

Something must have shown on his face, because she said, "I didn't think so. Duty before honor, right?"

"If I let you go," he pointed out, "I couldn't be sure whether you made it back to the States all right or not. Your stepfather might have other plans. Does my concern make me dishonorable?"

"No," she admitted quietly, her fingers folding and unfolding the edge of her napkin. "I knew you were too honorable to be working for him or Tony. I should have guessed you were a cop."

"I left the force months ago to find Tony," he told her. "I'm not going back." The words surprised him, although he realized the decision had been creeping up on him since he'd arrived on Isla Linda.

"What are you going to do?"

"I haven't decided yet. I've been a bit preoccupied." He grinned wryly. "Right now, the most important thing—for both of us—is to shake Tony out of hiding. No matter how we have to do it."

"What's going to happen to him when we do?" she asked.

"Concerned about him? He's a slimeball, Carly."

"You don't have to tell me that," she said. "He used me."

"No one gets used without permission," he returned, his voice harsh as he thought of the ways Tony might have used her.

"That's not fair," she said, tears making her eyes sparkle.

"You've always played the part of the victim, haven't you, Carly? Led astray by bad males, from high school troublemakers to Tony. And of course, it was never your fault."

She stood, her motions jerky and abrupt. "I don't have to listen to this. I'm ready to go back to the hotel now."

Dan stood, too, clenching his hands on the back of his chair, trying not to weaken as he saw her brush away a tear. From now on, they both depended on his strength.

Carly led the way into the hotel room, stopping in surprise at the changes that awaited them. Smithy had converted the room into a command center, complete with a portable computer and a fax machine. Two other men, also agents, judging by their short haircuts and dark suits, stood along the wall as though they needed nothing so sissy as a chair. Carly felt herself shrinking at their assessing gazes. She wanted to turn and lean into Dan's chest, soaking up his strength.

Between a rock and a hard place, she thought without humor.

"We've been checking a bit further into Arthur Wright's background," she heard Smithy tell Dan. "He's got more than a little gambling problem. He had to leave the U.S. when he ran into trouble in Vegas. He's a bit of a con artist himself."

"Then he could be Tony's contact in Isla Linda."

"Either him or Paolo Guzman, like you said."

Carly felt a wave of shock hit her. "Paolo? You must be joking."

Smithy turned to stare at her, as if he'd just heard the nightstand start talking. Then he looked at Dan, who spoke.

"Carly, until we know for sure who Tony expected to see in Isla Linda, we have to suspect everyone. Paolo's a powerful man on the island. He owns the hotel where Tony took you."

"Arthur Wright owns part of it, too," she said. "And part of the housing development on that side of the island."

Dan and Smithy exchanged glances. "You didn't tell us this before."

"You didn't ask," she pointed out. "Only Mexican citizens can own land, so Paolo and Arthur have some kind of arrangement."

"How did you know about this?" Smithy asked suspiciously.

"Paolo told me. We're like family. I don't know if I can lie to him."

"Then hope he doesn't ask any questions. If he does, let Dan handle it. Is there anything else you haven't told us?"

Four pairs of eyes watched her expectantly, and she felt like hiding in the bathroom again. At last Dan broke the silence.

"I think Carly just proved that she can help us in this planning session," he pointed out.

This time she wasn't booted from the room. As the hours passed and the sun shining through the window grew hotter, she reluctantly provided them with information about Isla Linda, everything from tide schedules to gossip about its residents. As the sun finally faded, she reminded herself it was worth it to catch Tony. They sat on the floor—Carly, three FBI agents, and Dan—grouped around the remains of a large room-service meal as though they were college dorm mates staying up late to coach one another before an exam or exchange the latest campus gossip. Only this was no party...

"Well, that's it then," Smithy said. "You two will use your friendship with the Wrights to arrange some kind of fishing trip. We'll go over the details again in the morning. In the meantime—" he turned to Carly "—I tried getting a female agent here, but Roy and Tom were the only ones available for this bit of extracurricular duty. I hope you don't mind."

"I do mind." Carly was tired of being surrounded by men, especially these men, with their hard eyes and quick reflexes.

"I'll watch her," Dan inserted before she could protest farther.

"I did hope you would volunteer," Smithy said, grinning. The other agents filed out. "I don't have to tell you the kind of trouble you'll be in if you lose her," she overheard Smithy tell Dan on his way out. She heard Dan's rude rejoinder and knew he was about as happy with the situation as she was.

"I noticed you didn't eat much tonight," he said after Smithy finally cleared out. "Are you tired of room service? We could probably find a restaurant still open somewhere."

"Aren't you afraid I might give you the slip?" she said, using her best Cagney imitation.

"Quit joking. I'm sorry they treated you like you were some kind of gun moll." He began picking up the crumpled napkins and dirty plates that were scattered about the room.

"I don't care about them." She looked at him pointedly, hoping he'd get the hint.

He did. He stopped cleaning up and said, "What do you want from me, Carly?"

"Trust. When they looked at me, they were seeing Tony Williamson's mistress. What do you see, Dan?"

"I see a woman who's too smart to get involved with a man like Tony Williamson. What did he do to draw you in, anyway?" He shoved the trash into the small wastebasket next to the bed.

Carly watched him, sensing the anger behind his jerky movements, and wondered if she could ever make him understand. If anyone epitomized the word *confidence,* it was Dan Turner. He acted like a man who had never had a doubt in the world.

Or was he able to hide his doubts from others? She remembered his earlier confession that he didn't know what he was going to do after quitting the force, and that memory helped her admit, "I didn't have a lot of confidence in myself until I learned to take care of myself here in Mexico." She stood and walked to the sliding glass door, trying unsuccessfully to find the moon. No lunacy tonight, she told herself.

"Tony encouraged me," she went on. She turned to face Dan, who was standing next to the bed. "No matter what else you say about him, Tony is a clever man. He knew so much about investments—"

Dan snorted, and she changed tack. "I was flattered that he thought I was intelligent enough to understand the things he taught me. And I trusted him."

"Enough to go off to Mexico with him?"

"I didn't know he was married. He lied to me."

His smile was crooked. "Liars seem to be your type, don't they?"

Carly faced him across three feet of space that seemed more like miles. As she looked at him, she acknowledged to herself all the things that she loved about him. At the same time, she rebelled at the thought that she'd inherited her mother's bad luck with men.

From now on, she would have only good luck, she vowed. She would start getting what she expected, by God, and from here on out, she expected the best.

Chapter Ten

This was going to be a long week.

Dan clenched the rail of the ferry boat. *Week?* Hell, it might take several weeks to lure Tony into the trap the FBI had planned for him. And all the time Dan was caught in a trap of his own—headed for an island paradise with the woman of his dreams, who acted as though she'd rather be at the dentist's having a root canal. *Without* Novocaine.

Ever since leaving Cabo San Lucas, she'd been civil to him, nothing more. He realized how much he missed her smiles. Instead, she treated him like . . . like he was the kind of jerk who would lie to her, then try to make her feel as though she was the one who couldn't be trusted, a voice inside Dan's head taunted.

Only a half hour ago, she'd been laughing and joking in Spanish with a deckhand when Dan had reminded her that they were supposed to be lovers. She had turned on a false sweetness—touching his arm, smiling suggestively—that had driven him all the way up here to the prow of the boat, where he stood and watched the island grow closer and remembered when such gestures from her weren't an act.

He spotted a pair of small figures on the dock and recognized two of Paolo's daughters. They shyly returned his wave before running toward the small cluster of buildings that could loosely be called "town."

Off to tell Papa, he guessed, dreading the encounter with Paolo, but knowing it was best to get it over with soon. He only hoped Carly was a better actress than her efforts had proven so far. He turned abruptly to look for her and found her standing farther down the rail, her expression unguarded. The look of vulnerability on her face propelled him toward her, like a hummingbird to a flower, he thought, remembering the afternoon they had spent together watching the tiny birds at the cove. By the time he reached her, her polite mask had slipped back into place.

"Look, Carly, I don't know how many more times I can say I'm sorry."

"It's not your apologies I want," she said.

He refused to be drawn into another argument. He didn't want to argue with her, just kiss her senseless and drag her off to bed. Impatience lent a harshness to his words as he said, "I have a feeling Paolo will be waiting for us. If you want to catch Tony, you'd better make this look convincing."

"You know how I feel about lying to Paolo."

Exasperated, he reached out and pulled her toward him. "Then don't," he said, before covering her mouth with a firm kiss. His lips gentled when he realized she was responding to him. God, how long had it been since he'd kissed her? Only days, but he felt like a man who had been caught in the desert for weeks without water. He opened his mouth and drank deeper.

They jumped apart at the loud blast of the horn that announced the ferry's arrival. He held her close in the crush of passengers debarking for the island. Among them were strong young men with knapsacks slung over their shoulders, women leading clusters of children, even a small white goat that bleated plaintively.

"Where did all these people come from?" he asked, speaking into Carly's ear so she could hear above the noise that surrounded them. "There must be more people on board this boat than there are on the entire island."

"It's a feast day tomorrow," she told him. "A local celebration. Most of these people grew up on the island and went to the larger cities for jobs. They're back to honor the island's patron saint."

Dan guessed the goat's fate and sympathized with it as he spotted Paolo standing at the edge of the dock, his arms crossed in front of his broad chest and his expression dark as a thundercloud.

They descended the ramp when it was their turn, and Paolo was there to take Carly's hand from Dan. He could barely keep up with Paolo's rapid Spanish.

"Are you all right, Carlita? Are you coming back to stay?"

"I'm fine," she said, bussing his cheek. "Dan and I had a little fight, that's all. But he followed me to Cabo, and we spent the whole weekend patching things up, didn't we?" She smiled brilliantly at Dan.

"Huh? Oh, yes," he added quickly, realizing he'd been staring stupidly at the warmth coming from those blue eyes. The love shining out of them seemed so genuine, he could almost forget this show was for Paolo's benefit and believe it was for him alone.

"Then I am happy," Paolo said, reaching for Dan's hand. The ferocity of Paolo's grip and the warning look he shot Dan over Carly's head indicated anything but happiness. "You will join us for the big feast in the square tomorrow, no? Help us honor our very own Santa Teresa?"

"Of course," Dan said. He shot another sympathetic glance toward the goat, as it tripped noisily along the dock toward shore, completely unaware of its fate. Dan wondered how he'd gone from being an acceptable suitor to dog meat as far as Paolo was concerned.

He pasted a smile on his face as he watched Carly become engulfed by Lupe and Paolo's chattering brood of children. Yes, it was going to be a long week.

Dressed in her most modest sundress, a knee-length, pale blue cotton, Carly stood next to Dan as the feast day procession wound its way down the dirt street to the small village's stucco *iglesia*. The bell rang in the tower, reverberating around the buildings and out across the water, and her heart felt as light as the sound.

Last night, Dan had shared her cottage. He'd slept on the floor and not in her bed, but she hoped to amend that soon. It was only a matter of time before he acknowledged his feelings for her, she told herself.

Portraits of Santa Teresa de Mar, the local saint, were held high above the dark heads of the crowd, almost appearing to dance to the music of the guitars and flutes as the procession made its way toward the church. The islanders wore their best clothing, crisp white cotton shirts or dresses, embroidered with yarn that rivaled the colors in the bouquets of flowers that were everywhere Carly looked.

A few of the expatriots had come from the other side of the island to observe the local tradition, among them Edith and Arthur Wright. She felt a jolt of alarm go through her at seeing them.

They waved, and Carly waved back, her eyes scanning the crowd for Tony. If only she and Dan could get this deception over with soon. But seeing Tony here would be far too easy, not to mention unlikely. If Tony had managed to stay away from the island this long, it would certainly take more than a local religious observance to get him to return. Even if he did, there was still the major problem of getting him out of Mexican territory and into international waters.

As the last celebrants filed through the carved wooden doors of the church, Carly pulled a lace mantilla over her short hair and started to follow. Dan stopped her with a hand on her arm and bent to speak to her.

"The Wrights are gesturing for us to join them." His voice tickled her ear. Indeed, Arthur and Edith were waving madly. Carly stiffened, and Dan must have mistaken her resistance for refusal.

"You can pay your respects to Santa Teresa later. Remember, the sooner we can get to Tony, the sooner we can put an end to this charade."

Carly's spirits sank, the last of her joy in the day completely fading away. She followed Dan to where Arthur and Edith stood, hoping the dread that felt like a lead ball in her chest didn't show on her face.

"We haven't seen you two for a while," Edith said, her smile teasing. "Off *touring* somewhere, were you?"

"As a matter of fact, yes. Carly and I were in Cabo San Lucas, getting to know each other a little better." Dan squeezed her hand, and Carly returned the pressure, holding on as if she were drowning and he was her rescuer.

"Cabo? How *romantic,*" Edith gushed. Carly noted the look of speculation on Arthur's face, and tried to school her features not to show her disgust.

"Did you stay at the Princesa?" Edith asked. "It's so elegant."

"Er, no, we found a quiet little place a few blocks from the ocean," Carly said. "It was very—" Dan squeezed her hand in warning "—pleasant," she finished.

"We'd be so *delighted* to have you join us for lunch. Wouldn't we, dear?" Edith shot a critical look at her husband, and Carly realized Arthur hadn't spoken a word since she and Dan had joined them.

"On the other side of the island, of course," Edith added quickly. "I'm sure everything over here is closed up tight for this celebration." Carly heard a patronizing note in Edith's voice. She realized she was becoming highly critical of people she once considered her friends. She didn't like it at all, and she wondered if Dan had needed to be this way with everyone when he was a cop. If so, no wonder he didn't want to rejoin the force.

"Actually, Paolo and Lupe are expecting us at their table for the feast celebration," Carly said. "Everyone in the village brings something for the feast. We're eating in the square by the church." She nodded toward the gaily decorated tables.

"But I'm sure Paolo and Lupe wouldn't mind if you joined us," Dan added, increasing the pressure on Carly's hand until she felt like stomping on his foot in retaliation.

"Then it's settled. We'll join you, instead," Edith said.

"Excellent idea, my dear," Arthur said, speaking for the first time. "I always enjoy chewing the fat with Paolo."

At Arthur's words, Carly no longer noticed the pressure on her hand. Arthur and Paolo couldn't be co-conspirators, she prayed. It seemed as though every single friend she'd made since coming to Isla Linda—people who had sheltered her and sustained her—had turned out to be false.

The rest of their conversation went past her as the four of them joined the throng leaving the church and heading for the long dining tables in the square. Lupe's eldest, Maria, quickly ran to get two more chairs for Arthur and Edith. The meal began after a brief blessing from Father Martinez, the circuit priest who'd made a special trip from La Paz for today's occasion.

Dishes of fragrant, spicy food were passed from table to table, as though the entire village was one big family. In a sense, it was—nearly every person seated at the table was a cousin or an in-law of some sort. Instead of feeling like an outsider, Carly felt a sense of communion with every member of the village and vowed to make time to go to the *iglesia* later by herself to thank Santa Teresa.

She passed along heavy pottery dishes of hearty bean stews, crusty breads, meats in flavored sauces. Her own contribution to the feast was a colorful fruit salad with a lime-and-honey dressing that Lupe had taught her to make. Dan solicitously helped her to select the tastiest morsels from each dish. She knew it was all part of the act, and she suppressed the urge to tell him that she'd been feeding herself since she was five years old. At one end of the table, the older Guzman daughters giggled and whispered behind their hands, their dark eyes going from Dan to Carly and back.

Carly hid an amused smile behind a glass of lemonade. If it wasn't for Arthur and Edith, the day would be perfect. But their presence added an awkward note every time Edith proclaimed how "quaint" this or that was, or whenever Arthur wrinkled his nose at a dish that was too simple or too spicy for his tastes.

At one point during the meal, Edith was trying to engage Lupe in conversation about how to make mole sauce, and Arthur was attempting to talk business with Paolo. In turn, Paolo was trying to question Dan—not very subtly—regarding their trip to Cabo.

"I'm glad the cantina is closed tonight," Carly intervened as she leaned back in her chair. "I'm too full to wait on tables."

"But surely you do not plan to work now that you and Dan are *novios,* eh?" Paolo commented.

Carly looked over at Dan to see if he had understood. Judging by the discomfited look on his face, his Spanish was up to the translation for fiancés. She nearly laughed aloud as he said stiffly, "She'll continue working until my paintings start to sell."

"A woman should not support her *esposo,*" Paolo argued. The Spanish word for husband caused Carly to sober instantly. She wondered how Dan was going to field this one.

"Since Carly and I aren't planning to marry for a while, we thought it best to keep things the way they've been," he said. Paolo looked about to argue, and she could feel the tension go out of Dan's body when Arthur changed the subject back to business.

"So tell me, Paolo," he ventured. "How do you feel about investing outside of the island?"

Carly didn't hear Paolo's response, which was lost in a fresh round of chatter as a tempting variety of desserts started making their way around the tables.

Later, while Maria and Magdalena cleared the table, and Dan organized a softball game among the other children, Paolo brought up the subject of Carly's love life again.

"That other man—you had a lucky escape. Never mind that he got away. He was no good. But maybe this man you will keep, eh?"

"Maybe."

"Then you must do things right. It is not right that you are living together as man and wife when you haven't spoken your vows before God."

"It's the way people do things now," she told him calmly. "They take the time to get used to each other, to decide if marriage is right for them or not before making their vows."

"Do you love him?"

"Yes," she said honestly, watching Dan show a teenage girl how to hold the bat to bunt.

"Pah. Then what is there to decide? Love is all."

"Not always," she said. "Sometimes loving someone isn't enough."

Paolo shook his head and exchanged a significant glance with Lupe. "You'll see. Leave it to me. Everything will be fine."

It took several moments before Dan realized that the pounding echoing through Carly's cottage was not in his head, but coming from the direction of the front door. It ceased momentarily, leaving a silence filled with the sound of the running shower.

Dan groaned and slowly rose to his feet, casting an evil look down at the pile of afghans and blankets where he'd slept for the second night in a row. Smithy insisted that he watch Carly every minute, including the nights, so while she curled up in her comfortable little cot, he'd been banished to the floor. He'd considered hauling his own cot in, but feared Paolo would be sure to notice its absence when it came time to relet Dan's cottage.

Even bone-tired from the baseball game he'd organized yesterday afternoon, Dan had a hard time sleeping. But why blame the floor? he thought, on his way to the front door. He heard the water stop running in the bathroom seconds before the pounding started in again.

He grumbled, "I'm coming," before yanking open the door to reveal Paolo, standing on the doorstep dressed in the suit he'd worn at yesterday's celebration. Beside him was the priest, Father Martinez.

Dan stood sleepily, wishing he'd taken the time to pull on a shirt over his jeans. The priest's dark eyes took in his state of undress, from his bare feet on up, although his gaze slid away before meeting Dan's.

"Who's at the door?"

Three pairs of masculine eyes focused on Carly, dressed in a thigh-length robe and toweling her short hair. She was developing a bad habit of appearing in public half-dressed, Dan thought grumpily.

"Oh, good morning, Paolo, Father."

Dan saw the priest look down at his shoes and mutter something in Spanish. Paolo's scowl was as dark as his suit. It disappeared when he turned to Carly. "I have good news. Father Martinez has agreed to marry the two of you before he returns to La Paz. Come with us now to the *iglesia.*"

Dan was instantly wide-awake. Carly glanced at him, her blue eyes filled with wicked amusement. He shot her a look of gratitude when she told Paolo, "l don't want to be married in a rush. I want a big wedding, with the banns read, and I want to wear a white dress."

Gratitude was changing rapidly to alarm.

"We have time for that later," Paolo said dismissively. "The padre is only here for a short time."

"But we'll have to return to the States in order for the marriage to be legal," she argued, while Dan was beginning to wish he had ignored the knock in the first place.

"At least you can be married in the Lord's eyes," Paolo argued. Dan shuffled his feet uncomfortably, hoping Carly could manage to dissuade Paolo, who appeared implacable.

"But Paolo, Dan has been a perfect gentleman." He shifted again, hoping he was the only one who heard the edge in her voice as she pronounced the word *gentleman*. "Look." She swept an arm toward the pile of blankets. "He's been sleeping on the floor."

The priest let out a shocked exclamation, and Paolo began a rapid flow of words in Spanish. Carly held her own, but the look she cast Dan was desperate. He realized that there was only one way out of this.

He had to trust Carly's judgment regarding Paolo and come clean about this masquerade. "Father, will you excuse us for a moment?" he asked as he signaled to Paolo. "Won't you step into my office?" He swept his arm toward the broad expanse of sand, and Paolo followed him.

As they walked along the deserted beach, Dan told Paolo about the FBI's plan to catch Tony Williamson. It was clear that Paolo still didn't approve of the arrangements, but he brightened when Dan reminded him that Tony would pay for what he'd done to Carly.

"That man is a bad one. Pah." Paolo spit.

"What do you know about Arthur Wright? Carly said you're partners."

"He has much money, but he spends more. Because of him I am able to do things for the island, to make jobs for people. But he has bad friends."

"Is Tony one of Arthur's friends?"

"Who can say? I saw him only the one time he came here with Carly. I wanted to hit him that night for mistreating such a beautiful woman."

Dan tried to steer Paolo back on track. "How do you think we could find out if Arthur knows Tony?"

"Ask him."

Dan was beginning to have serious doubts about Paolo's contributions to their scheme. "Too risky," he said.

"Arthur keeps trying to get me to invest more money. You heard him at the feast yesterday. But I will not work with those men he calls friends."

"Do you think Tony might be one of the partners?"

Paolo said, "Perhaps."

"Do you think you could persuade Arthur that you'd like to meet the other partners before deciding on an investment?"

Paolo smiled. "Certainly."

"There's a catch." Dan explained about having to get Tony into international waters.

"The solution is very simple," Paolo said. "Arthur likes to gamble. I will insist on a fishing trip and a friendly game of poker with his friends."

Dan looked up to find that they had walked all the way to the marina. Since they were so close anyway, he accompanied Paolo the rest of the way home. They refined the plan at the Guzmans' house over glasses of Lupe's freshly squeezed lemonade. Father Martinez was there, too, after walking back from Carly's by himself. He left the Guzmans' home reluctantly, obviously fearing that many more souls besides Dan's and Carly's were in danger.

"Be careful of moving too fast," was Dan's final warning to Paolo. "Arthur might think it odd that you changed your mind about spending money outside of Isla Linda."

"I will see him at the cantina tomorrow. He will bring it up himself," Paolo said with a grin.

As Dan walked back toward the cottages, the sun was getting low in the sky. This was going to be so much easier than he had expected. *Like leading a goat to the slaughter,* Dan thought.

Chapter Eleven

"You go home. I'll help Paolo finish up," Dan told Carly. She looked exhausted, her eyes larger and bluer than usual, and he felt a surge of protectiveness at the sight. He was used to feeling that way about her now. It no longer frightened him, although he wouldn't allow himself to feel anything more. Most of the time, he tried to think of her the way he thought of Janie...as a sister. Sometimes it even worked.

It had been a week since the festival of Santa Teresa, and Carly had waited on tables here at the cantina nearly every night. Dan did as much as he could to hasten an end to this limbo they were in, playing chess with Arthur whenever the older man suggested a match, hinting about the fishing trip as often as he dared. But nothing seemed to work. While one part of him wanted to get this ordeal over with as soon as possible, another part cherished every minute longer that he was able to spend with Carly.

"You'll be home soon?" she asked, so tired that she swayed on her feet.

"Sure," he told her, fighting the urge to go with her now. He wanted to walk home with her in the moonlight, to feel the damp sand on his bare feet, to follow her inside the cottage and spend the rest of the night holding her in his arms. "I'll be home soon," he repeated, noting how easily the word had come to them both.

Home. He watched her let herself out the door, then poured himself a shot of straight tequila. He'd need this and more to be able to sleep tonight, to quench the desire that was eating away at his insides. By letting her go back to the cottage on her own, he was violating Smithy's order to stick to her like glue, but any closer and he would be in her bed.

And why not, he thought, frustration burning in him as strongly as the unaccustomed straight alcohol. He drained the last of the fiery liquid and stood, hesitating when he realized his intention. He nearly jumped when Paolo came up behind him and slapped him across the back.

"I'm glad we have this chance to talk," he said, and Dan hoped the older man couldn't read minds. "In private. *Mano a mano,* eh?" He grinned and Dan smiled back with a considerable lack of enthusiasm.

"Carly is a beautiful woman, no?"

"No, I mean, yes, she's beautiful," Dan agreed, knowing where this conversation was headed and wondering if Paolo would come after him if he left for the back door right now.

"She is also—how do you say this in English?—*fragile.*"

"Fragile. Same word, we just pronounce it differently," Dan said, his smile weak.

"*Sí.* Fragile. And I am like her father." His jovial look disappeared, and his hand tightened on Dan's shoulder. "If you do anything to hurt her, I will tear you apart with my hands."

Dan stared into Paolo's eyes. If the threat had come from any other man, it would have been laughable. Dan was taller, heavier, fitter, with the training of the police academy and the lessons of the street behind him. But he knew Paolo meant every word.

Had Carly managed to delude Paolo, too? Or perhaps she really was as innocent as she appeared, something he wanted to believe more every day. The possibility wasn't so far-fetched after all, Dan thought as he stared into Paolo's implacable brown eyes.

"Do you remember when Carly came to Isla Linda?" he asked, wanting to hear Paolo's impressions of that evening in greater detail.

"I was there when she arrived with that—" He spit out a Spanish colloquialism that Dan was probably fortunate not to understand. "She was so innocent. Any man could see how shocked she was when he tried to share her room. I found another room for him, of course," Paolo said. "He left the next morning, and she cried for two days. Then she saw that newspaper and learned how he had cheated her. I can't wait to see this man get what he deserves."

"But she must have known he was married." Dan spoke unconsciously, half protest, half question.

Paolo halted his motion of wiping off the bar. "She is beautiful, and you do not see her," he said, shaking his head. "You do not deserve her love." He turned to enter the back office and Dan followed, holding out his palm to keep Paolo from shutting the door in his face.

"She . . . did she tell you that she loves me?" he demanded, wondering what need drove him to hear the words from Paolo. When they were in Cabo together, Carly had told him that she'd *thought* she was in love with him, and he assumed that he'd lost her regard a hundred times over since then. But if she had told Paolo since then that she loved him . . .

"Does she say she loves me?" he asked again.

Paolo stared at him. "Why do you ask me? Why not ask her? You and Carly must talk to each other."

Before Dan could pump Paolo for any more information, he found himself staring at the cantina's back door, closed firmly in his face.

Carly turned over onto her back and shaded her eyes against the sun reflecting off the water, smiling when the sound of children's laughter mingled with Dan's deeper chuckles.

Another week had passed, two weeks now since the festival. As they waited to hear from Arthur and Edith, Carly and Dan had settled into a routine that excluded his "painting." The cover story had been mostly for her benefit, anyway. Afraid that Arthur and Edith might ask to see paintings they would surely recognize, Dan had given Paolo the two canvasses for safekeeping.

Instead, they now filled their days with the lazy pleasures of paradise: sunbathing, beachcombing, swimming. Carly went to the cantina at sundown as usual, and Dan went with her every night. On the surface, little had changed, but underneath, the pressure built like a brewing volcano.

Last night at the cantina, Carly had overheard Dan remind Arthur of his promise to take them out on the *Mirabella*. Arthur had replied, as he always did, "I'm working on it."

She could feel the frustration building within Dan, although anyone else watching him would never guess that he was anything but a happy-go-lucky beach bum. Especially this afternoon.

Like a pied piper, he'd amassed a following of village children. They'd made effective chaperons over the last two weeks, and sometimes Carly wondered if Paolo had planned it that way. The villagers smiled and nodded their approval every time they spotted the group of children with the young couple, while Carly and Dan were left with nothing to do but exchange heated glances over the children's dark heads, then look away as though nothing had passed between them.

Carly watched from the shade of a large manzanita bush as Dan and his devoted followers played on the beach a few yards away. Today he was teaching them to play volleyball, using an old fishing net stretched between two palm trunks. The sand "court" was bordered by rocks and seashells to make in-and-out-of-bounds, but the children ignored the boundaries and resisted the concept of scoring. For them, the real game meant sending Dan hurtling after balls halfway to the water, chortling with laughter when he landed facedown in the sand.

As Carly watched, it happened again. When Dan stood and exaggeratedly spit sand from his mouth, Carly found herself giggling along with the children.

Dan glanced her way, and her laughter ceased. He still reminded her of a pirate, rugged and bold in his cutoffs, with a bandanna tied rakishly around his forehead. But she knew so much more about him now than she had when he'd arrived on Isla Linda over two months ago. And the more she knew, the more she was certain they were meant to be together.

The problem was in convincing Dan.

The nights were the worst. He had taken to helping Paolo close up the cantina in Carly's stead, coming home long after she should have fallen asleep. But try as she might, she never lost her grip on consciousness until she heard him enter the cottage. She would lie there and listen to him moving around in the darkness, longing to reach out and touch him, to guide him to her lonely bed. But she couldn't bring herself to do it, not as long as he still harbored a shred of doubt about her.

How could he continue to doubt her innocence? she wondered. Ever since they had started sharing the same cottage, he'd come to know her as well as she knew him. In one sense, they were like a married couple, familiar with each other's habits and personal tastes.

She knew, for example, that Dan didn't speak in the morning until he'd been awake for at least a half hour. And he was aware that she always had two spoonfuls of sugar in her first cup of coffee, but none thereafter. When it came to the deeper feelings and motivations that guided Dan's actions, however, she often felt she didn't know him at all.

Most of the time, they were considerate and even affectionate, like long-time roommates, but every now and then the feelings between them flared like a fire storm. At those times, Dan invariably retreated, leaving her feeling frustrated and rejected. They never referred to her "affair" with Tony, and the subject simmered between them dangerously, like a pot about to boil over.

She decided that Dan must be using his suspicions to keep himself at arm's length. Tony was just an excuse. It was something else that kept him from her, and now, as she watched him playing with all the enthusiasm of a child, she wondered if the key was in the bleakness of his own childhood.

"Dano, Dano, watch me," a little girl with black braids cried in Spanish. She attempted a serve that landed weakly behind the net. Dan dived for it anyway and pretended to trip, spinning in a circle and tangling in the net before landing dramatically on the sand. He was immediately overrun by little sun-browned bodies.

"Enough," he called out, sending the children into another round of giggles. "This is supposed to be a volleyball game—football was last week. Old Dano needs a rest." He poked his head up and shot Carly an imploring glance. "My Spanish isn't that great. Can you translate for me?"

Carly did, adding a suggestion that Lupe might be coaxed into making cold lemonade for them. The children swarmed away in a blur of arms and legs, and she mentally apologized to Lupe for sending the horde her way.

"What did you tell them?" he asked, standing and brushing the sand from his cutoffs. It was a hopeless battle since the gritty sand clung to him like a sugar coating.

"I said that you were a dirty old man," she teased. "I think you'd better dive into the water and wash off."

"Only if you'll come in with me." His eyes gleamed in invitation, and Carly didn't hesitate, diving into the water only seconds behind him.

"Have you been practicing?" she asked, catching up to him after a few solid strokes.

"A little. I don't want to go out too far with all the kids around, although most of them can swim better than I can," he admitted ruefully.

"That's still a wise precaution," she approved, slowing down to float for a while. The water felt soothing against her arms and legs, although it couldn't ease the ache inside her. Only Dan could do that, and he didn't appear interested.

"It's even hot in the water," he complained, floating on his back and staring up at the sky. "No wonder some people spend the afternoon in siesta."

"Why don't we try it?" Carly suggested lightly.

He didn't even look at her as he replied, "You go ahead. I promised Paolo that I'd help him work on that old boat of his father's. He's thinking of starting a charter business." He turned and started to swim toward shore, calling over his shoulder before he got too far, "I'll see you later at the cantina."

"Sure." With a feeling of exasperation, Carly watched his strong arms slice through the water. If only it were possible to teach people to love as easily as it was to teach them to swim.

When she arrived at the cantina hours later, she found Dan and Paolo toasting each other with celebratory beers. Arthur had called Paolo that afternoon to tell him the fishing trip was all set.

They would be leaving the day after tomorrow, but Arthur had been enigmatic about the route they would take. All he would tell them was that he had made arrangements to pick up several friends en route, business associates that he wanted Paolo to meet.

"It's hardly enough time to call Smithy and get things arranged," Dan complained as the three of them sat at the bar and waited for the evening's customers to start to appear.

"Perhaps that is why Arthur planned it this way," Paolo pointed out. Throughout the week, he'd been unusually pessimistic, maintaining that Arthur's continual delays meant trouble. "He might be on to us," he said, sounding like an actor in an old gangster film.

"Not a chance," Dan said.

"He doesn't even know Dan's last name," Carly pointed out. "There's no way he could put everything together and come up with the right explanation."

"Except through Tony," Dan countered. "If Tony sees me, he'll recognize me. On the other hand, he doesn't want to be recognized, either. If he's coming on this trip, I bet he'll be one of the business associates we pick up after we're already afloat."

"If he's coming at all," Paolo added gloomily.

Customers started to pour into the bar, and Carly reluctantly left the comfortable bar stool. It was a busy night, but her mind still found ways to worry about the fishing trip. Tony wasn't the only one who could be arrested in international waters, she realized. She felt as though she were being squeezed by a giant fist. She was so tense and nervous, she hardly knew what she was doing, confusing several orders and breaking three glasses. Jorge was puzzled, but Paolo watched sympathetically.

She was still lying awake after work when Dan returned to the cottage and settled into his bed on the floor. She listened to his uneven breathing and knew he was as sleepless as she. She wished she dared suggest that they keep each other company, but nothing would induce her to speak out, not after his rejection earlier that day. Even so, she wanted to feel his arms around her more than anything else in the world.

When she heard Dan get up and go out the door, she dressed in her white swimsuit, grabbed a towel and followed. He was sitting on the sandy beach, staring out at the sea. Above them, a silvery white crescent moon dangled in the dark sky like a woman's earring. She spread out her towel and sat next to him. They watched the surf wordlessly for a few minutes before Carly spoke.

"It's so calm and peaceful, isn't it? It doesn't seem fair that people like Arthur and Tony can come here to escape the consequences of their actions."

"Nothing seems fair anymore."

She recognized the tight frustration in his voice because it matched the feelings that had been pressing in on her all evening long. She murmured, "Including the way you're treating me."

"What do you mean?"

"You act as though I'm a leper. Like you have to force yourself to be around me," she said.

"We're together constantly, Carly. Smithy's orders, remember? I'm supposed to stick to you like glue."

"But we're rarely alone," she pointed out. "And when we are, it feels as though you're somewhere else. Take now, for example. You haven't even turned to look at me since I sat down. I know that, somewhere underneath all that disapproval, you care for me, even if you don't believe I'm innocent."

"I believe you didn't plot with Tony to steal the money," he said woodenly, as though he'd rehearsed the words.

"That's not what I'm referring to, and you know it. I think you're trying to convince yourself I went away with him even though I knew he was married. It's not true, Dan. Don't you know that by now?''

He didn't answer, and she said, "You're afraid to admit it, aren't you?''

He turned to face her, and his words cut her. "Maybe I am. You're not exactly the woman I'd bring home to meet my family. My sister..." He broke off. "Oh, hell. Even if it wasn't for Tony, or for all of this, I don't know if I'd be able to give you what you want.''

"Please, Dan." She edged closer to him and held a hand to either side of his face, looking into his eyes. "Try for me. All I want right now is for you to talk to me, to tell me what's wrong.''

With a deep sigh, he took her into his arms and proceeded to tell her why he was afraid. She'd heard it all before, the stories about how his parents used to rage at each other, but before she'd believed him when he said he was over it. It was obvious now that the scenes from his childhood still haunted him.

"I get angry sometimes, Carly," he confessed. "And it scares me.''

"We all get angry. There's nothing wrong with that. It was different for your parents.''

"How do I know it won't be different with me, too?''

"Trust yourself.''

"I can't. There's been too much conflict between us already.''

"I think that goes with the territory. Maybe when this is all over with..." Her words trailed away. Maybe with time Dan would learn to take a risk on loving someone, but they didn't have time. In two days, if everything went according to plan, she would be on her way back to Phoenix. Dan still hadn't decided what he was going to do.

For a moment, she wished Tony wouldn't show up for the cruise tomorrow, then realized that if he didn't, her chances at beating the embezzlement charges in court measurably decreased. It seemed as if there was no way out for the two of them.

She shivered, and Dan held her tighter. His arms were comforting around her, and she didn't protest when he leaned back. They ended up lying on her towel, staring up at the stars. They held each other like that until the sky began to lighten, watching the miracle of the new day as the sky changed from rose to orange before becoming a pure zircon blue.

Was this as much of Dan as she would ever know? Carly wondered. Or was two days enough time to change his mind? She glanced at his profile, and nearly started crying at the tension in his features. Did she dare allow herself to hope? She tried to find a calm space within her, blue and pure as the sky, knowing she couldn't risk disappointment once more.

It would be far easier to let go now, she thought, as she drifted into sleep.

Dan watched as Carly slept, curled on her side in the narrow cot. It was almost noon now, hours since they'd viewed the sunrise together and she'd fallen asleep in his arms. He had carried her inside and pulled the covers over her, glad she had a chance to catch up on sleep before going to work later in the day. For his own part, he knew he wouldn't be able to close his eyes until it was all over.

He left the cottage quietly and started walking along the beach. Only twenty-four more hours and Carly would have to return to Arizona, and he—

His thought ended as abruptly as if it had hit a brick wall. What would he do? He had no place to go, no job, no ties. With Tony's capture, his promise to his sister would be fulfilled. He might have to testify at the trial, but after that he was a free man. He still had plenty of money in the bank, money he'd saved up over years of double shifts and holiday duty, trading hours with cops who had spouses and families to go home to.

Home. There was that word again. He'd begun to think of Isla Linda as home, but he realized that was because of Carly. After she'd gone, he'd be no more at home here than anywhere else. He thought about taking the vacation he turned down every year. Maybe he'd even learn to paint. His grin faded at the prospect. He could move nearer to Janie and the kids, but that would feel like a substitute for the real thing, a family of his own.

He looked up from his inner debate and noticed his surroundings for the first time in several minutes. He realized he'd made his way to Hummingbird Cove. He paused, ready to turn away from the memories he and Carly had left here. Then a bright little bird whizzed by him, and he sat down on a rock to watch, as though he'd been enchanted by a leprechaun. He wondered if Isla Linda even had fairies. He'd have to ask the children.

But he remembered that after today, he wouldn't be spending his afternoons with the village children anymore. No more laughter, no more shared smiles. Then he realized it was Carly he was thinking of now, and not just the kids.

At least if they caught Tony, she would go free. She deserved to be free because she'd done nothing wrong, except fall for the wrong man. And this time he wasn't thinking of Tony Williamson.

"Hello."

He looked up, startled to find her standing beside him. "I didn't even hear you," he admitted.

"Some cop," she teased. "You looked lost in thought."

"Yeah, I guess I was. What time is it, anyway?" He moved over so she could sit beside him on the flat-topped rock.

"Almost two." He realized that he had been daydreaming for nearly two hours. "What were you thinking about?" she asked.

"I was wondering what I'm going to do after this," he told her. "I might stay here." The words surprised him, because he thought he'd already dismissed staying in Isla Linda from his list of possibilities. But now it seemed more right than any of the other options he'd come up with so far. Unless . . .

He glanced over at Carly, lovely as a fairy herself in the pale blue sundress that showed off the color of her eyes. Unless his impulse to stay was because he wanted to be here with his memories of her.

She turned and their gazes met. He felt as though he were falling down an endless tunnel. The familiar fear rose up in him again, and he knew the only way to quench it was to kiss her.

Did he dare? In the end it would only make things worse. He hesitated on the edge for what seemed like forever before he made a decision.

"We'd better go," he said, rising to his feet.

Chapter Twelve

The day of the fishing trip dawned partly cloudy and hot, but Carly felt a heaviness in the air. She couldn't be sure if it was the weather or if it was due to the sense of foreboding that filled her as she dressed in her orange bikini and covered it with a batik wrap-front dress.

"Are you almost ready?" Dan called. Even through the closed door, Carly could hear the edge to his voice.

"Two more minutes," she replied. She guessed he must be as jumpy and agitated as she was, although he'd never admit it. She'd barely been in the bathroom twenty minutes, and it was still long before they were supposed to meet the Wrights at the other marina on the expatriots' side of the island.

The fact that Dan was unsure of their exact itinerary meant a change in plans. And that, she suspected, was responsible for his tension. Sometime during the trip he would have to find an opportunity to contact Smithy from the yacht's radio, and hope that one of the three boats the FBI was using to patrol along the international waters boundary would be near enough to get to the *Mirabella* in time.

It would be up to her and Paolo to create a distraction so Dan could radio. Her fingers trembled as she glossed her lips with a sunscreen. She steeled herself and opened the door, stepping aside as Dan brushed past her, unshaven, his hair tousled.

The skin of her arm tingled where his bare chest had come into contact with it. She shot him an accusing glance, even though she knew how unreasonable it was to get angry at him because his touch affected her so much.

He stared at her reflection in the mirror above the sink. His voice was harsh as he said, "Don't, Carly. I was up all night going to hell and back thinking of all the things that might go wrong today. Don't make it worse by looking at me like that."

"Like what?" she whispered, her gaze dropping to his lips. He groaned and gripped the edge of the sink.

"Like a woman who's hungry for more than breakfast."

She looked away. "If the FBI arrests Tony today, I'll have to go back across the border with them, won't I?"

"You know you will. As soon as we cross into international waters, the FBI has jurisdiction. I've talked to Smithy about not arresting you, but he didn't make any promises."

"I'll go with them willingly. What about you—will you be coming, too?" she asked.

"I'm not with the FBI," he reminded her.

"I know. I thought maybe..." She could tell him how much she needed him beside her, but would he listen? His expression softened at the plea in her eyes.

"Let's just get through today, okay?"

"Sure," she said, her voice falsely cheerful.

While Dan showered, she kept herself busy packing a few necessities into her bright red tote bag: sunscreen, aspirin, aloe vera lotion. As though a headache or sunburn would make or break this day, she thought with wry humor.

"Ready?"

She spun around to find Dan watching her from the doorway, dressed in faded jeans and a white polo shirt.

She nodded, and he took the tote from her, hefting it two or three times before asking, "What have you got in here? A bowling ball?"

"I'm not sure," she admitted. "I just started throwing things in without thinking."

"Nervous?" he asked, reaching up with his free hand to massage her shoulder.

"Yes." The word ended on a sigh as she leaned into his touch. His strong fingertips kneaded the tenseness from her muscles, then gentled to rub between her shoulder blades. Just when she was about to collapse with pleasure, he removed his hand from her back.

"We're meeting Paolo by the cantina," he told her briskly. "The three of us will drive together to the other side of the island."

"Do you think Tony will be there?" she asked, mostly to make conversation as they walked to the car.

"Maybe. It's more likely that he's one of the men the *Mirabella* is stopping to pick up." He glanced at her assessingly as he opened the passenger door for her. "If not, we'll try to forget about it all and just have a good time. Don't worry. Everything will be fine."

"Of course," she said, wishing she believed it.

"There. That one is Arthur's yacht," Paolo said, pointing to a long, sleek vessel waiting at the end of the dock.

"Yacht? It looks more like a cruise ship," Dan said as they walked down the dock. "Ahoy," he called, waving as Edith appeared on the *Mirabella*'s deck.

She invited them to board, explaining that Arthur was still below, checking over the fishing gear the men would be using. "You're welcome to have a try, too," she told Carly, "although I must warn you that Arthur takes his sport very seriously."

"I'll sit this one out, thanks," Dan overheard Carly say as the women walked ahead.

Dan barely listened to the rest of their polite chatter as his gaze scanned the large deck. It would be easy enough to get to the main cabin without being noticed, he decided, but once inside, he'd have to duck or be spotted through the large glass windows. The radio must be somewhere in there.

He counted three discreetly uniformed crew members above deck. He also made note of distances and the amount of cover available. He started walking toward the steep staircase that led below deck. Before he reached it, Arthur's head and shoulders appeared in the square opening.

An expression of apprehension passed across Arthur's face when he saw Carly and Dan. Then his features relaxed into a jovial grin. He stepped onto the deck and slapped Dan on the back before leading him toward the railing.

"We're still setting a few things up down there in the galley. Fishing till sundown, poker later. How does that sound?"

"Great, except I'm not sure I have enough money for a high-stakes game," Dan said. He pulled his wallet from his back pocket and opened it, revealing the thick wad of cash that Smithy had sent, all counterfeit bills the FBI had confiscated during another case. A quick glance seemed to be enough to convince Arthur. He barely managed to conceal the greed in his gray eyes.

"Don't worry, we're all gentlemen. We'll work out something." He smiled. "We're taking on the other passengers in an hour," he said as the yacht pulled away from the dock. "We're not far enough out for the big fish yet, but let's get you and Paolo set up now."

"How about a tour of the *Mirabella* first?" Dan asked.

Arthur spread his arms in an expansive gesture. "You can see her all from here, except below deck, which you'll see later on. We'll set up our gear here," he told Dan, his hand gripping the railing. "I'll just go see what's taking so long."

As soon as he left, Carly joined Dan at the railing. The sun brought out the red highlights in her hair, and Dan wanted to bury his face in the silky strands. He reminded himself of the reason that they were here.

"Did you get the idea that Arthur doesn't want us going below?" he asked.

"Yes. I asked Edith if I could put my tote bag below, and she actually refused. So I stashed it under a deck chair," Carly said with a shake of her head. "Of course, we might be a bit paranoid," she admitted. "This could turn out to be nothing more than an enjoyable day on the water."

"I'd rather get it over with," he said grimly.

"Me, too." She sighed and looked out across the diamond-bright waves, giving Dan an opportunity to admire her lovely profile.

"Although I'd like to spend a day alone with you," he added, knowing their time together was coming to a close and wishing there was something he could do about it.

"Really? Or are you just being polite?"

Her words surprised him. "I enjoy being with you, Carly. That's what makes this so hard. Maybe we could see each other sometime when I get back to the States."

"You sound like the people in my office."

"What?"

"You know—the way some people say 'let's do lunch' even when they don't mean it."

"Ah, Carly." He looked around, wishing they were alone. The deck seemed to be crowded with people. Edith was supervising a crew member in the process of setting up a portable bar, while another carried armfuls of gear toward them. Paolo was staring in their direction, his eyes narrowed.

"I do care for you," Dan said, his voice low. "You know that. Can't we finish this conversation later?"

"We may not have a later," she pointed out before leaving him to join Edith and Paolo.

Dan turned to stare out at the water, wondering if he was defective in some way. Maybe he was missing the gene or chromosome that made it possible to leap headlong into deep water, to fall in love without reservation, to be intimate with another human being. It wasn't like loving your parents or your sister, or even like choosing a friend. It was a free-fall with no parachute and no guarantees.

He was still watching the bow split the waves in front of the yacht when Arthur came up behind him, slapping him across the shoulders and startling him.

"We're almost to our stop. After that, it's out to sea. Are you ready?" he asked, and for a moment Dan's mouth went dry, until he realized that Arthur meant if he was ready to fish.

"Sure," he said, trying to drum up a believable level of enthusiasm. At any other time, he would have looked forward to a day outdoors. But today he was preoccupied with worry—over whether or not Smithy would find them, over what would happen to Carly. Fishing seemed like silly nonsense in comparison, even the prospect of tangling with a creature that weighed as much as he did.

He joined the others as they welcomed aboard the newcomers, three middle-aged men whose smiles, as they were introduced to Paolo, reminded Dan of crocodiles. These were the hopeful investment partners, and Tony Williamson wasn't among them.

Dan's gaze met Carly's, and his disappointment was reflected in her eyes.

Men, Carly thought as another chorus of excited shouts rang out from the other side of the yacht. She looked to Edith for support, but the older woman was stretched out on a lounger beside her, fast asleep, her limbs oiled liberally with sun lotion. Despite her age, she wore a white two-piece swimsuit, and Carly had to admit that Edith looked smashing.

But her hostess had neglected her duties, napping on and off since their light lunch. Carly was bored to tears at the prospect of sunbathing all afternoon long. The men's voices rang out again, and she shook her head. At least someone was having a good time. Ever since Arthur had reeled in a four-foot-long sailfish about an hour ago, Paolo and Dan had been acting like a pair of rabid fishing enthusiasts, without care in the world.

But Carly was tired of the noise and the sun and the heat.

She looked over at Edith again, still sleeping. The tight knot of males didn't even notice as she stood up and walked across the deck to the staircase that led below. The crew was nowhere to be seen, and she knew none would be the wiser if she went down below for a short rest.

As soon as she was below deck, she started opening cabin doors, smiling at the memory of the old children's tale about Goldilocks. She stopped when she found a small bedroom that looked "just right," loosened the wrap around the tie of her batik dress and lay down on top of the blue quilted spread. She sighed in pleasure at the blissfully cool air coming from a vent on the ceiling.

She must have drifted off to sleep because a stealthy noise made her jump and open her eyes. The noise came again, a footstep, and she knew she wasn't alone. Someone stood in the open doorway.

She squinted at the backlit figure, trying to identify him. "Dan?"

The figure stepped into the room. "Sorry, Carly, but lover boy is preoccupied right now." He closed the door to the hallway, but she already knew who it was, even before his smooth features became visible.

"Tony."

"You remember. I'm flattered."

She sat up, clutching the edges of her dress around her with one hand, searching with the other for the tie belt. She didn't take her gaze from the blond man standing only a few feet from the bed.

"Oh, don't be modest, Carly. Not when I've waited so long to see you again."

She held the edges of her dress tighter and told herself to be calm. "Have you been on board since we left Isla Linda?"

"The whole time. As soon as I saw who your boyfriend was, Arthur and I agreed that I should save my appearance for the business segment of the evening, when we *reel* in the *real* catch." He laughed at his pun. "It's been a very boring trip, I'm afraid. Until now." He stepped closer.

He laughed at her involuntary movement backward. "Come now, Carly. Don't tell me you're not as anxious as I am to finish what we started a year ago, huh?"

"If you touch me, I'll scream," she warned him. "Then everyone will know you're here."

"My dear, everyone does know. Except for lover boy, of course."

"Paolo, too? *No.*" She felt a wave of shock and revulsion. It doubled when Tony grabbed her by the wrist.

"You wanted it badly enough once," he said, his pale brown eyes scanning her face before moving downward. "What's the matter? Is your new lover the jealous type?" His features hardened. "Dan Turner can't make you as happy as I did."

"You and I were never lovers," she spat out, yanking her wrist from his grasp. She wasn't about to play the victim a second time to this man. He looked surprised at her resistance, and she wondered if his memory was failing him.

"Regrettably. But we will be." He advanced toward her, and she rolled off the narrow bunk, landing on the floor in a heap.

She scrambled to her feet and tore open the door, running into the hallway screaming for Dan. Her cries were lost as more shouting broke out above deck. She reached the staircase with Tony following closely at her heels. He grabbed her by the elbow, but before she could attempt to shake him loose, she felt something hard and unforgiving at her back.

"One more inch, one more sound, and you won't be able to climb up these stairs or any others."

She froze, then looked up helplessly as Paolo's unmistakably stocky form blocked the square of daylight. He looked down and saw Tony. "Carlita?"

"How could you?" she whispered, staring up at the latest of her betrayers.

Paolo started toward her, then froze at Tony's shouted warning to stop. Tony rapped out instructions at him, pulling Carly out of the way as he said, "Down the stairs. One word and she dies."

He shoved the gun against her back, and she winced involuntarily.

Paolo came down the steps, his eyes wide with fear. Carly watched in confusion as Tony herded him into the cabin and blocked the door from the outside.

"No sounds, *comprende?*" he warned Paolo through the door.

"You lied," she accused, suddenly understanding. "Paolo didn't know you were here. He has nothing to do with any of this." She realized that she'd made things that much easier for Tony by believing his lies.

He tipped back his head and laughed. "I've been hiding out in some hot hellhole south of the border for a year," he said, his voice almost a whine. "There isn't even anything to spend my money on."

As Carly listened, she realized it wasn't money that motivated Tony. It was power—manipulating other people's lives. By embezzling two million dollars, he'd inadvertently put an end to his clever cons and machinations.

"What are you going to do?" she asked. He laughed again, and she realized his year in exile had unbalanced him.

"I'm going to have fun," he said, waving the gun in the air. "I'm going to gamble, I'm going to make love to a pretty woman. And—" his voice hardened "—I'm going to make sure that Dan Turner doesn't follow me anymore. I'm going to have enough fun to last through another year of hiding. But then, this time, I'll have you with me, won't I?"

Carly closed her eyes, swallowing back her fear and nausea. The only hope she could cling to was that Tony didn't know Dan was working with the FBI. If Dan had a chance to get to the radio....

But Dan didn't even know Tony was on board the yacht.

She wondered about the other three men above deck. How would they react to a madman? My God, would it be up to her and Dan to stop them all? She tried to focus on Tony's words as he whispered instructions into her ear, but with the gun barrel pushed firmly into the hollow below her earlobe, concentration was difficult.

"I want to hear you beg me to make love to you, Carly. And then I want Dan Turner to come down here and find you in my arms."

Revulsion went through her in waves even more fierce than the ones rocking the boat. *"No."*

A loud crack drowned out her horrified denial, and the floor beneath their feet tipped sharply starboard, knocking her into Tony and sending them both sprawling to the floor. She recovered first, scrambling to her feet and running for the staircase.

She could hear Tony's labored breathing behind her, combined with shouts from above deck. The boat bucked and tossed, and she had to grip the handrails tightly in order to keep going up. When her head and shoulders cleared the opening onto the main deck, confusion greeted her eyes.

Crew members and passengers bumped into one another as they stumbled back and forth with the rocking of the boat. The sky was a threatening gray, split with lightning and thunder.

"Un chubasco," she heard one of the crew shout, his voice rising above the terrified yells of the others.

Her gaze sought Dan as she pulled herself onto the deck. She saw him staggering toward her and yelled, "It's Tony. Get to the radio."

She barely got the words out before she felt a hand close over her arm and the familiar touch of cold metal against her ear.

"Everybody stand still," Tony ordered.

People stopped where they were, all except Arthur, who took a step toward Carly and her captor, his palms outspread.

"You, too," Tony warned him.

"But we're in the middle of a storm, Tony," Arthur said reasonably. "It came out of nowhere. Let the crew do their jobs or we'll all go down."

"Not until I get a boat."

"You'll never make it in a smaller boat, Tony." This time it was Dan who spoke. "Just give me the gun, and you can stay with us or go, if you really want to die that way."

"No." Tony's refusal was almost petulant.

The wind tore at Carly's hair. She could hear another roar—an engine—sounding through the howling wind. Her gaze flew to Dan. Did he hear it, too?

His attention was on Tony as he slowly advanced across the slick deck. Carly felt the gun leave her temple and watched in horror as Tony pointed it at Dan.

"No!" she screamed. Her cry was lost in a loud explosion and a shattering blow that knocked everyone to their knees. Carly and Tony rolled over and over across the deck. Tony still had hold of her arm, and she pulled hard to free herself.

She succeeded—only to realize that there was nothing at all holding her anymore. *She was falling overboard.*

She felt water closing over her head, and everything after that was like a dream. Dan's voice penetrated her senses, and she wondered if she was hallucinating until she saw him fighting the waves to reach her.

"Hold on, sweetheart," he shouted, then everything went black.

"Is she all right?" Dan stared at the small, blanket-covered figure lying on the *Mirabella*'s deck. One of Smithy's men bent over her, helping her to cough up the water she had swallowed.

Her eyelids fluttered open, and her gaze searched the crowd of people that stood over her until it landed on him. He dropped to his knees beside her, letting the blanket he was supposed to wear to guard against shock fall from his shoulders.

"I'm fine," she told him, her voice husky from coughing. "Sure glad you know how to swim." She grinned weakly, and he could feel a wetness on his face that wasn't from the light rain that was still falling after the passing of the sudden storm.

"I love you," he told her.

Her smile grew stronger. "I have witnesses," she said, her gaze going around the group that included Smithy, several of his agents, the crew, Edith and Arthur Wright, a hand-cuffed Tony Williamson, and a slightly green Paolo, who'd suffered more than any of them in his below-deck prison.

"Good," Dan told her, barely noticing as someone settled the blanket over his shoulders again. "Then I won't have to ask you twice to marry me."

"What?"

"Marry me," he said, forgetting he was supposed to phrase it like a question. He waited for the falling sensation to come over him again, but he'd apparently faced his fears and conquered them in a split second as he'd gone over the side of the yacht after Carly.

"When the storm hit, we tried to find you. I nearly went crazy," he told her. "I can't live without you, Carly."

"Sure you could," she teased, sitting up with a little help from Smithy. "But you won't have to. I'm sticking to you like glue," she said, reminding Dan of Smithy's instructions.

He tipped back his head and laughed.

Epilogue

Four months later

Carly walked slowly up the sidewalk to the Maricopa County courthouse building in downtown Phoenix. Dan held her hand tightly, and she knew he was much more nervous than she was.

Now that the moment of truth was here, she was really quite calm.

Then she spotted the small cluster of reporters and photographers standing by the glass entrance doors. Her nervousness returned full force as they rushed toward Carly and Dan, microphones extended. The reporters' voices all blended together:

"Miss Dawson, Miss Dawson."

"How does it feel to be a multimillionaire, Miss Dawson?"

"Is it true that your stepfather, Robert Daimler, has applied for bankruptcy protection? That the two of you aren't speaking?"

"Any comments on Tony Williamson's sentencing?"

She felt Dan's arms go around her protectively, and she found the presence of mind to smile at a prematurely graying reporter, whose notebook dangled from his hand. He smiled back.

"Congratulations on your marriage, Mrs. Turner."

"Thank you, but it's not legal yet," she told him, laughing. "That's why we're here."

Camera bulbs flashed and voices rose again as Dan held the door open for her. She walked through the lobby to the elevator, smiling widely as the doors slid shut on all the commotion.

"Alone at last," Dan said, bending to kiss her. He was handsome and a little unfamiliar in his sober gray suit and red tie. She wore red, too, a silk dress with a matching jacket that made her feel wonderfully brazen.

"Nervous?" she asked.

"Nah, not after the first time," he said, his smile wicked.

She pictured the wedding ceremony they'd celebrated just four days earlier on Isla Linda. The entire village had turned out to wish them well. Children with scrubbed, smiling faces had showered Carly and Dan with flowers and rice the moment they walked through the doors of the *iglesia,* while the bells pealed sweetly through the village. Carly had worn the traditional Mexican wedding dress, white cotton with tiny pleats, trimmed in lace.

The ceremony four days ago might not have been strictly legal, Carly thought, but it was the marriage of her heart. Today was just a formality.

They were making their union official with a civil ceremony here in Phoenix before heading back to the island, where Dan and Paolo had already outlined plans for their charter boat company. Her trust money would help them get started, but Carly had plans of her own, too. A school for the children and a full-time priest for the village, for starters.

She gripped Dan's hand tighter as they entered the judge's chambers.

"Ready?" she asked him as the judge approached, solemn in her dark robes. "You could still back out, you know."

"And risk facing Paolo coming after me with a shotgun? Not a chance," he said. His expression grew serious. "I'd marry you every week for the rest of my life, Carly Dawson."

The judge cleared her throat. "Shall we begin?"

*   *   *   *   *

SMYTHESHIRE,
MASSACHUSETTS.

Small town. Big secrets.

**Silhouette Romance invites you to visit Elizabeth August's
intriguing small town, a place with an unusual legacy
rooted deep in the past....**

THE VIRGIN WIFE (#921) February 1993
HAUNTED HUSBAND (#922) March 1993
LUCKY PENNY (#945) June 1993
A WEDDING FOR EMILY (#953) August 1993

Elizabeth August's SMYTHESHIRE, MASSACHUSETTS—
This sleepy little town has plenty to keep you up at night.
Only from Silhouette Romance!

HE'S MORE THAN A MAN, HE'S ONE OF OUR

Fabulous Fathers

INSTANT FATHER
Lucy Gordon

Gavin Hunter had always dreamed that his son, Peter, would follow in his footsteps. Then his wife left him, taking their child with her. When fate reunited father and son six years later, they were strangers. And with the boy's mother dead, Gavin blamed the child's guardian, Norah Ackroyd. But soon Gavin found loving Norah was easier than blaming her.

Share Gavin's triumph as he wins the heart of his young son and the love of a good woman in Lucy Gordon's INSTANT FATHER, available in August.

Fall in love with our **Fabulous Fathers** and join the Silhouette Romance family!

FF893